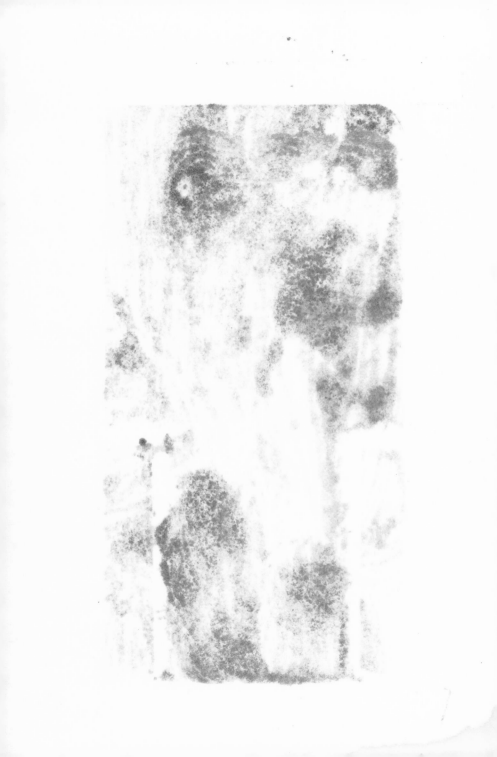

The
Doomsday Marshal

Also by Ray Hogan

TRAIL TO TUCSON
THE HOODED GUN
BLOODROCK VALLEY WAR
RECKONING IN FIRE VALLEY
MAN WHO KILLED THE MARSHAL
JACKMAN'S WOLF
CONGER'S WOMAN
MAN WITHOUT A GUN
HONEYMAKER'S SON

The Doomsday Marshal

RAY HOGAN

DOUBLEDAY & COMPANY, INC.

GARDEN CITY, NEW YORK

1975

All the characters in this book are fictitious,
and any resemblance to actual persons, living or
dead, is purely coincidental.

Library of Congress Cataloging in Publication Data

Hogan, Ray, 1908-
The Doomsday Marshal.

I. Title.
PZ4.H716Do   [PS3558.03473]   813'.5'4
ISBN 0-385-08446-3
Library of Congress Catalog Card Number 74-25106

For . . .

EDMUND MILLS CLAYTON, M.D.
. . . *pioneer southwestern physician to whom I am indebted for many things.*

1

He was a tall man, well constructed, and as he rode down the single street of Colorado's Boston City that early spring morning and angled toward the hitchrack fronting Town Marshal Rufe Whitaker's office, there were few who did not notice him.

It was not so much his general appearance—flat-crowned, plainsman style hat, gray shirt with silver buttons, leather vest, cord pants with the legs tucked inside scarred, stovepipe boots—but the aura of lethal efficiency that clung to him like a grim halo. A gunslinger or a special breed of lawman; it was apparent in the hard, straight set of his mouth, the flat-lidded colorless eyes with their line of overhanging dark brows, and in the way nothing seemed to escape his cool attention.

Deputy Linus Kirby, standing in the doorway of the jail with the aging Whitaker, viewed the newcomer's approach with a smirking tolerance.

"Tough-looking sonofabitch, ain't he?"

The marshal stirred. "Best you mind your tongue, boy," he murmured.

"What for? He's just a lawman like plenty of others, ain't he?"

"Lawman, sure—like others, no."

"Bull! He gets wet in a rain same as I do. Way some

folks act when his name gets spoke makes my belly heave. You'd think he was some kind of a ring-tailed stem-winding wonder!"

"Was you a little older and a lot smarter you wouldn't be saying something like that," Whitaker said quietly, and stepped out onto the landing fronting the building.

The newcomer had pulled up to the rack, halted. Sweeping the small crowd gathering behind him with a sharp, appraising glance, he swung off the big chestnut he was riding and came slowly about.

Whitaker said: "Ain't no point in asking, you'll be John Rye."

A stir went through the onlookers. Rye settled himself squarely on his feet in the loose dust, nodded.

"And you're Rufe Whitaker. Last time I saw you was up Kansas way."

The old lawman smiled, pleased at being remembered. "Was me all right. Didn't figure you'd recollect the time . . . This here's my deputy. Name's Linus Kirby . . . I'm mighty glad you've come."

Rye made no answer. Someone in the crowd said in a hoarse whisper, "It's him for sure—the one they call the Doomsday Marshal."

Another, carefully quiet, added, "Got the looks of a killer, ain't no doubt of that."

The corners of Rye's mouth tightened slightly, and then shrugging he moved toward the two men on the landing. He had a slow, easy swing to him as if every part of his muscular body was loose, ready to respond instantly to any emergency.

"You got Braden ready to go?"

Whitaker bobbed, brushed at the stubble on his chin. "Want to see him?"

"Later," Rye answered, and, stepping by the marshal and his deputy, entered the cluttered office. "Let's get off the street."

"You expecting to get a bullet in your back?" Kirby wondered in an amused tone.

"Something I'm always looking for," the lawman said, pausing in the center of the room. Turning, he faced the deputy. "Be obliged if you'll see to my horse."

Anger flickered briefly in Kirby's eyes, and then he wheeled, crossed to the doorway. "One of you jaspers take Mister Rye's horse to the livery stable," he directed curtly. Coming back around he nodded to the tall man. "I ain't nobody's flunky."

Rye, ignoring the deputy, halted beside the desk placed in the rear of the office, glancing indifferently at a door to its right that apparently led to the jail cells. As Whitaker circled around to him, he reached into an inner pocket of his shirt, revealing as he did the slim hilt of a knife carried below an armpit, and drew forth an envelope.

Dropping it onto the desk, he glanced at Whitaker. "The warrant for Braden's release," he said in his flat, spare way. "Papers from the U. S. Marshal's office telling you who I am are there, too."

"Sure won't be needing them."

"Best you look them over, anyway," Rye replied, and shifted his cold attention to Kirby. "Something about me that's bothering you?"

At the blunt question the deputy drew up. "Just getting

me a good look at you, Rye," he said boldly. "Ain't never seen no killer-marshal before."

Rufe Whitaker glanced up hastily, eyes anxiously searching Rye's expressionless features.

"He don't mean nothing by that, Marshal," he said hurriedly. "Young—ain't got much good sense yet—"

"Don't go backtracking for me!" Kirby cut in angrily. "I don't need no busted-down old man—"

John Rye's arm lashed out. The back of his hand caught the deputy across the face, sent him staggering into the wall.

"You've got a loose mouth, boy," he said quietly. "That old man as you call him was laying his life on the line for folks long before you were even born. You'll never see the day when you'll be half the lawman he is."

Hatred glowing in his eyes, Kirby recovered his balance, forearmed away the blood trickling from his crushed lips. His shoulders came forward slightly and his right hand began to lower toward the pistol on his hip. At once Whitaker stepped in front of him.

"Don't be a danged fool, Linus!" he snapped, and then nodded apologetically to Rye. "It's all right, John. I'm getting sort of used to people talking that way. Like I said, he don't mean nothing bad."

The frozen, chiseled lines of Rye's features did not change and there was neither challenge nor quarter given in his manner. Abruptly the deputy wheeled, stepped through the doorway onto the landing. Ignoring the several questions thrown at him from the crowd, he stalked off down the street.

"Linus's a mite upset," Whitaker said, following the

rigid figure of the young lawman with his eyes. "Was wanting the job of taking Luke Braden back to Yuma Prison hisself. Figured it'd make him a big man, I reckon."

"Or a dead one," Rye said dryly, shrugging.

The old marshal grinned. "Being young he never looked at it that way. . . . Mind telling me your plans so's I can sort of get things ready?"

Rye crossed leisurely to the door, glanced out. A scuffle of some kind was taking place in front of a saloon named the Marigold, and the assemblage that had collected before the jail was hurrying to witness the new attraction.

"Be riding out with him in the morning."

Whitaker sighed deeply. "Suits me fine. I'll be mighty glad to get him out of my jail. Way things are going in this town it won't be long 'til there ain't nothing but his kind left. Decent folks are all pulling out."

"Why?"

"All them people that come here figuring to set themselves up and do farming found out plenty quick they'd been suckered. This just ain't farming country. Ain't no rain. Flat busted, they're moving on. It was for them the town sprung up and with them gone, it's dying. About all we've got left is a bunch of drifters and outlaws—there's a gang called the Jennings that're sort of running things. They will for sure soon as I light out."

"You leaving soon?"

"Couple of months—ain't no need for a lawman no more. That's part of what's galling the deputy. Figured on hunting hisself a job when he got to Arizona and using this here Braden thing as a recommendation."

"This Jennings gang—they friends of Braden?"

"Reckon you mean will they give you trouble when you haul him out of here? No, I don't think so. They don't know him that good. Fact is, Braden's a sort of a newcomer. Blew in here with his wife—"

"Wife?" Rye echoed, leaning back against the doorframe and folding his arms across his chest. "Didn't know he had one."

"Yeh, a right pretty woman. Come here together a month or so ago. Somebody said they'd just got hitched over in Las Vegas. Only friends they can name are a few they've made in the Marigold."

"She hang around there, too?"

"Yeh. Deals faro—same as Luke was doing when I got the word to pick him up."

Rye resumed his contemplation of the disturbance in the street. Two more men had joined in the fray, which showed promise of becoming a general free-for-all.

"If there's going to be trouble for you, I expect it'll be her doings," Whitaker said, settling into his chair. "Already made it known she ain't letting you take Luke to Yuma."

"Anybody else talking the same line?"

"Nope, only her. You ever buck up against a woman in something like this before?"

"First time—but it won't make any difference. Handle her the same as if she was a man. All alike to me," Rye said indifferently. He was quiet for a long minute, his hard features immobile, eyes vacant. Then, "I'd like to have a look at her."

"Sure, she'll be there in the Marigold," Whitaker said, rising.

"Can a man get a bite to eat there?"

"Yeh. Grub ain't the best—better down at Ma Ferguson's place—but it'll pass. . . . Like to ask a favor of you, Marshal."

John Rye's brows lifted questioningly. "Yeh?"

"It's about the deputy. Like as not we'll be running into him. If he gets to aggravating you and pushing you, I'll take it kindly if you'll just sort of look the other way, let me handle him. He's a good boy—just needs watching over."

Rye shrugged. "He's all yours," he said, and stepped out onto the landing.

2

The street in front of the jail had cleared, almost everyone with nothing better to do now gathered in the area near the Marigold Saloon. The scuffling and fisticuffs appeared to have tapered off with several of the participants standing about dusting themselves while they talked with friends and bystanders.

Whitaker, following Rye into the open and moving to his side, squinted at the crowd and wagged his head as they started for the saloon. Somewhere beyond the town in the direction of the towering, snow-capped Rockies, several gunshots flatted through the crisp, clear air. They drew attention from no one.

"This here Boston City could've been a mighty fine place to live," the old lawman said dispiritedly, "had things gone right. Turning into a hellhole now."

Rye nodded, half-shut eyes scanning the street, probing the shadowy passageways that lay between the buildings, the open doors, the dusty, streaky windows. Many of the structures were vacant, the original occupants, facing up to failure, and moving on, having left their property to the drifters and vagrants.

"There many people still around?"

"Three, maybe four hundred. Was double that once."

John Rye's step slowed, a tightness drawing his features

into flat planes. And then as the squat figure of a man emerging from one of the shacks became distinct, his long body eased and the sudden tenseness disappeared. It had come and gone in only brief moments but it had not escaped Whitaker's attention.

"Somebody you figured you knowed?"

The lawman's shoulders moved slightly. "Thought so."

"Could've been. Place is fair crawling with outlaws. Jail I've got wouldn't be half big enough to hold all the wanted men hanging out here—did I have to jug them."

"Could start. Lock up the ones you've got wanted dodgers on—maybe keep the town from going completely to hell."

"What'd be the point? Ain't no reason to try and save it 'cause there ain't no need for it now. And far as locking up a bunch of them jaspers, their friends'd have them busted out before I could turn my back."

"Didn't break out Luke Braden—"

"Like I told you, he ain't got no friends worth mentioning. Now, you try jugging one of the Jennings crowd or somebody like them and it'd be different."

They reached the saloon, and stepped up onto the wide porch at its lower end. The rumble of conversation ceased almost immediately at the arrival of the two lawmen, but the attention of the crowd was not on Whitaker but on John Rye.

Aware of the impression he created, the tall, somber marshal crossed slowly to the center of the board gallery, paused, wheeled deliberately. Facing the gathering, he allowed his glance to travel over it, touch each person with a sardonic assessment. Then, equally deliberate, he half turned, laid his arm across Whitaker's shoulders, and coming about continued on for the entrance to the Marigold.

The gesture had been one of pure showmanship, but the warning, so subtly presented, could not be missed: Rufe Whitaker was his good friend and anyone harming the elderly marshal would answer to him.

As they stepped into the noisy, crowded building hazy with smoke and heavy with the smells of tobacco, kerosene, stale beer and whiskey, and unwashed bodies, Whitaker hesitated, then looked up at the taller man.

"I'm obliged to you—"

"For what?" Rye said bluntly, and began to make his way toward the long bar placed against a back wall.

The hubbub gradually diminished as he progressed and when, with Whitaker at his side, he reached the counter, a near complete silence had settled over the room. Rye bucked his head at the round-eyed bartender.

"For me—whiskey," he said, and glanced at the old lawman.

"Same," Whitaker responded.

The man behind the counter produced glasses and a bottle, poured the required drinks and stepped back.

"Be a dollar."

Whitaker reached into his pocket. Rye brushed him off, took a quarter eagle from his vest and flipped it to the waiting barkeep.

"We'll be wanting another."

Taking up the shot glass, and with the same cool indifference he'd shown the crowd in the street, Rye pivoted slowly. Resting his elbows on the edge of the bar, he returned the pressing stares of the Marigold's patrons with a quiet disdain.

At once they began to pull away, resume whatever had been occupying their attention when he had put in his appearance. A small, almost bitter smile cracked his lips as he took a pull at the raw liquor. There likely wasn't a man there who wouldn't enjoy putting a bullet into his heart; only the force of his personality and the fear of failure were keeping them from trying. He knew none of them by name but they were the counterparts of many others scattered throughout the frontier and they hated him not for anything he'd ever done to them but for what he was and what he stood for.

"Here's luck," Whitaker said, raising his glass.

"*Salud*," Rye answered, and tossed off the remainder of his drink.

Coming back around, he beckoned to the bartender. "Once more, friend," he said, sliding his empty glass toward the man. "How about something to eat?"

"Got venison steak, and the trimmings."

"That'll do," the lawman said, waiting while the barkeep refilled Whitaker's glass also. "It suit you, Marshal?"

"I'll pass," Rufe said. "Done had my meal."

"Be one order then. Bring it over to that table in the corner."

"Sure. Won't take long."

"Rye—"

The tall marshal's head came up slowly at the sound of Linus Kirby's voice. Hands flat on the counter, he did not turn.

"There's your boy," he said quietly to Whitaker.

In the sudden hush that had fallen over the saloon the old lawman swore deeply. "Been wondering when he'd show up," he said, coming about.

"Rye—you hear me?"

"He hears you," Rufe Whitaker replied, "and it's only me standing here that's keeping him from putting a bullet in your fool head! Now, you get on back to the jail and look after the prisoner. Hear?"

Someone in the crowd laughed. The silence broke and the babble of voices resumed. John Rye remained motionless and then his shoulders relented slightly as Whitaker was again beside him.

"He's gone. . . . Sure hate doing that to him in front of all these folks, but he's just got to learn . . . Let's go get comfortable."

Rye pulled away from the counter, led the way to the table in the rear of the room and settled down. Rufe took the chair at his side, still muttering under his breath. Activities in the saloon once more were in full sway with several card games in progress, a full line at the bar and half a dozen or so couples rocking and stomping about on the small dance floor to the barely audible music of the piano.

"You see Braden's wife?"

Whitaker threw his glance out into the smoky room, shook his head. "Nope, sure don't. But she's around somewheres."

Rye grunted, downed his second glass of liquor in a single gulp. "You know if he's got a horse and gear?"

"Yeh, pretty fair-looking black gelding. Keeps him at the livery stable. Gear'll be there, too."

"I'll be wanting to look him over, see that he's in shape to travel."

"You can do that when you're through eating," the lawman said, and paused. An altercation of some sort had broken out on the far side of the room—shouting, the crash of a splintering chair, a volley of cursing. Rufe Whitaker did not stir.

Rye grinned at the marshal's disinterest. It was evident he intended to waste none of his time on a lost cause.

"Where you headed when you leave here?" he asked.

"Dodge, I reckon. Can always get myself a job there as a jailer. . . . About all I'm good for anymore . . . Here comes your grub—and it's Zoe Braden bringing it."

Rye glanced up. "Thought she was a dealer—"

"She is. Must've talked Abe into letting her be your waitress."

The lawman smiled enigmatically, settled his narrowed eyes on the approaching woman. She was young, probably not yet twenty, and well built. In the saloon's murky light her skin appeared dusky and her dark brown hair, gathered loosely about her face and flowing down onto her shoulders, had a reddish tinge. Her eyes were a definite blue and were accented by shadowing, and there was a touch of rouge on her lips. She was wearing a yellow dress cut low at the neck but unlike those worn by the other girls in the Marigold, it reached almost to her ankles.

"A real looker, ain't she?" Whitaker commented in a low voice.

Rye's silence was his agreement as he waited while Zoe Braden crossed to where they sat, a platter of meat, potatoes, greens and light bread in one hand, a thick mug of coffee in the other. Beyond her nearby patrons were looking on in a sort of eager expectation.

Setting the food and drink on the table, the girl took a knife and fork from a patch pocket in her dress, dropped them noisily beside the plate, her eyes pushing at him steadily.

"So you're him," she said scornfully, falling back a step. "The big, tough lawman everybody's so scared of."

Rye picked up the knife and fork, began to work on the venison.

"Well, you're just a two-bit killer, far as I'm concerned," Zoe continued icily. "As soon deliver your prisoner dead as alive."

John Rye paused. "I cut my cloth to suit the man I'm dealing with," he said coldly. "Whether he gets where I'm taking him alive or not's up to him. . . . This talking go with the meal or am I getting something extra?"

"I'll tell you what you're not getting!" she flared. "You're not getting to Yuma Prison with Luke—with my husband. I'll promise you that."

Rye resumed his eating. A man at the bar tittered, hushed instantly when the lawman glanced at him. Whitaker shifted nervously on his chair.

"Why don't you go on about your business, Missus Braden, leave the marshal be? He's only doing his job."

"My husband is my business!" Zoe snapped. "And this fancy gunslinger who likes to have folks call him the Doomsday Marshal's got no right to come here, take Luke—"

"He's got every right. Luke's an escaped criminal,

sentenced to hang for murder. Marshal Rye was sent to fetch him."

"He's got no authority here in Boston City—"

"Where you're wrong, missus. Kind of job he's got gives him the say-so anywhere in the country. A Special U. S. Marshal, that's what he is. President Hayes signed his papers personally, I'm told."

"I don't give a damn if Lemonade Lucy signed them, too!" Zoe shouted. "He's not taking Luke back to hang— not unless he kills me doing it."

John Rye paused, looked up at her. "That's just what I'll do, lady, if you get in my way," he said softly, and again turned back to his meal.

Zoe Braden stared at him for a long breath, eyes smoldering. Suddenly she whirled and hurried off into the crowd. A cheer went up from somewhere in its depths, but it was halfhearted, died quickly when no one else took it up.

Rye, watching her move off through his brows, a hard smile on his lips, toyed with a bit of the venison at the end of his fork. When she had disappeared into the pack of customers, he shifted his attention to Whitaker.

"One hell of a lot of woman," he said admiringly. "Don't seem the kind that would tie up with a man like Braden."

"Everybody makes mistakes," the old lawman said.

Rye returned to his food, finished off most of what was on the plate, washed it down with the coffee. The mug empty, he glanced toward the bartender.

"How much I owe you?"

"Be another dollar."

The lawman dug the necessary coin from his pocket,

dropped it onto the table. "Living's a mite high around here," he observed, rising. "Those friends of the Bradens ever show up?"

Whitaker again scanned the Marigold's patrons, once more shook his head. "Sure don't see them."

"Well, forget it. Like to have that look at Braden's horse. Expect to pull out with him in the morning at first light. Want to be sure everything's ready."

Whitaker got to his feet, concern showing on his lined, weathered features. "Maybe you shouldn't've said that so's others could hear," he murmured. "Ain't no sense in asking for trouble."

Rye only shrugged, and said, "Let's go see that horse."

3

An hour later, with the day turned unseasonably warm, John Rye returned to Boston City's jail with Marshal Rufe Whitaker still with him. He had examined Braden's horse carefully, concluded the black was in good condition and ready for the long ride to Yuma Prison.

As they entered the small office Deputy Kirby, slumped in the chair behind the desk, looked up sullenly. His lower lip showed a bluish thickness, and his eyes were filled with a brooding anger. Whitaker stepped in close to him.

"Good time for you to go get yourself a bite to eat, son," the lawman said gently. "Anybody come by wanting to see the prisoner while I was gone?"

"Nobody," Kirby replied stiffly, and, jaw clamped tight, he rose, crossed to the door and stamped out into the street.

"Pride of his is sure festering," Whitaker said thoughtfully. "Kind of wondering about him."

Rye gave it a few moments' consideration, made an indifferent gesture with his hand. "Send him off somewhere. Get rid of him 'til after dark."

"Yeh, reckon I could do that," the lawman said, scratching at his stubble. "One of the homesteaders—the Collinses—that ain't gone yet, picked up a couple of stray horses a while back. Been aiming to go out there and have a look at the brands. Can send Linus."

"Do it," Rye said shortly. "He's not old enough to trust and I don't want to be worrying about him shooting off his mouth—or getting in my way."

Whitaker continued to rub at his jaw. "You figuring on doing something?"

"I'll be riding out with Braden soon as it's full dark."

"Tonight? Thought you said it'd be in the morning."

"What I said there in the saloon and what I'll be doing are two different things. . . . Like for you to saddle up Braden's horse and load up his gear and bring him around back. My chestnut, too."

"Now?"

Rye stirred impatiently. "Wait 'til dark. Don't want anybody seeing you do it."

"I see. That's why you're wanting the deputy out of here. What about grub?"

"I'll make what I've got do. Be another town where I can get what I'm short. Need another canteen, however. My extra took to leaking. Be obliged if you'll pick one up for me."

"Sure thing. I can make out like I'm buying it for myself."

Rye nodded his approval. "I'll have a look at Braden now."

"You'll have company doing it," Whitaker said, glancing out into the street. "His missus is coming—bringing him something to eat. Them jaspers with her are them friends I was telling you about."

Rye moved around behind the lawman's desk, leaned

against the wall. Moments later Zoe Braden, a plate covered by a napkin in her hands, entered. She flicked Rye with a contemptuous look, nodded to Whitaker and marched up to the door leading into the area behind which lay the cells. Halting, she turned to the older man.

"Well, are you going to open up?"

The marshal, ring of keys in his hand, was watching the three men outside on the landing. "You all just do your waiting right there," he drawled, and crossed to where the girl stood. Lifting the napkin, he checked the food, squinted at her.

"Ain't never searched you yet, don't much favor doing it now, but I'm asking—you carrying a gun anywheres on you?"

"Of course I am, Marshal," Zoe replied flippantly. "Got one under my dress. You want to see it?"

Whitaker flushed, shook his head. Inserting a key in the lock, he opened the heavy door, allowed the girl to enter. Leaving it ajar, he turned to Rye.

"Know what you're thinking; I should've searched her."

"I would have," the tall man said. "Been a few lawmen got themselves killed acting the gentleman like that."

"Ain't never tried nothing before. Can't see no reason why she would now."

"Plenty of reason," Rye corrected, moving to the window facing the street. "Her husband'll be on his way to hang in the morning, she thinks. This'll be about her last chance to help him. . . . Who are these three friends she brought along?"

Rufe stepped up to the dusty glass through which Rye was now observing the men. "That short, heavy one with the scar is Walt Crow. Rode in with Luke and his missus when they come from Las Vegas. Yellow-headed one's some kid that sort of took up with them. Name's Tom Horn. Other'n, the curly-haired one's called Curly Hyde. Pretty handy with that iron he's packing. All of them are, far as that goes."

"They friendly enough with Braden to go out on a limb for him?"

"Could be but it's my thinking they're more interested in his woman."

"Enough to side in with her in trying to break him loose?"

"Yeh, I do—it all depending on what they figure to get out of it from her—which could be a-plenty."

Rye started some comment, closed his mouth abruptly as Zoe Braden came back through the inner door. Eyes straight ahead, she crossed to the jail's entrance, and stepping out onto the landing, rejoined her waiting friends. Together they struck for the Marigold, the girl a step or two in front of the three men.

"She bring him supper, too?"

"Nope, just dinner, but being his last night she'll maybe want to do some visiting."

"Tell her no if she does," Rye said, moving toward the cell room. "She puts up a holler, say she can drop by in the morning. . . . Now, lock me in here with Braden. You can go pick up that canteen I'm needing while you're waiting."

Whitaker nodded. "Sure thing. Won't take more'n ten minutes."

"No hurry," the tall lawman said as the door swung shut behind him.

Shoulders flat against the wall John Rye settled his attention on the man behind the bars of the first cell. Luke Braden was somewhere in his mid-twenties, a dark, spare man with a clipped mustache and an engaging smile.

"Been wondering what you'd look like," he said, pleasantly. "Them sending the big Doomsday Marshal after me sure does make me proud. Like to say—"

"Start taking off your clothes," Rye cut in coldly.

Braden stared. "What's that?"

"Strip—and hand your duds to me through the bars."

Braden began to unbutton his shirt. "Don't see no reason—"

"You don't need a reason," Rye said coldly. "That goes for anything I tell you from now on. Get it into your head once and for all—I'm taking you back to Yuma Prison. Whether you get there alive or dead's strictly up to you."

"I can see where they get what they call you," Braden mumbled, passing the shirt to the lawman. "We catching that noon stage tomorrow?"

Rye was carefully going over the outlaw's shirt, making certain it concealed nothing. Satisfied finally, he tossed it into a corner.

"No stage—we'll be in the saddle," he said, taking Braden's broadcloth trousers and beginning to put them through close inspection.

Luke wagged his head dolefully. "That's a hell of a long ride, Marshal."

"For a man going to a hanging it oughtn't to matter," Rye said unfeelingly, and threw the pants aside. "I want the boots, the socks and the drawers."

Braden swore helplessly, completed his disrobing. Rye went over each article painstakingly, added them to the pile in the corner. He had found nothing concealed in any of the pieces of apparel.

"Now just sit back quiet," he said. "You'll get your duds back when it's time to go."

"You saying I'm to set around here buck naked all night?"

"Just what you're going to do. Better enjoy it. Once we start, you'll be wearing leg chains and handcuffs."

There was a thumping on the door. Whitaker's voice came through the thick panel.

"It's me—Rufe. I'm back. You done in there?"

"All finished," the tall lawman answered.

He was glad Braden had given him no trouble and thus voided the necessity of his entering the cell and accomplishing the search for hidden weapons by force. Luke was an agreeable sort and showed a pleasant, friendly manner to the world—one that might be considered charming. John Rye was not fooled by such; Luke Braden was a cold-blooded, ruthless killer.

The door swung back and Whitaker stood framed in its opening. He stared at Braden, mouth sagging, and then shifted his attention to Rye.

"Got you your canteen—and I sent the deputy out to the Collinses," he said. "You searching Luke for a knife or something?"

Rye nodded. "He was clean."

"Could've told you that," the old marshal said. "His missus wouldn't've slipped him something—not after she give me her word. . . . Ain't you going to let him dress?"

"Later," Rye said, turning toward the door. "I'll be going over them again. Once had a man hide a gunny-sack needle in the seam of his pants—another took the handle off his razor, hid the blade under the innersole of his boot. Taught me never to take a chance. He'll get his duds just before we head out—right after dark."

"Dark!" Luke Braden shouted as Whitaker closed the door. "You said it'd be tomorrow!"

Rye smiled. "Just goes to prove you can't trust anybody nowadays," he said dryly.

4

It was yet an hour until first light when Zoe Braden left the shack at the edge of town where she and Luke lived. Clad now in boots, a pair of her husband's old pants and one of his shirts, a wool jacket, a bright yellow scarf holding her dark hair in place—which was further protected by a narrow-brimmed hat secured by a thong looped under her chin—she was ready for the trail.

It shouldn't take long to free Luke; she ought to be back in Boston City well before sundown and in plenty of time to report for work as usual at the Marigold. She was not bothering to take any large amount of food, only some bread and meat, ground coffee beans with a small pot and cups—sufficient to satisfy the needs of herself and the three men who had agreed to accompany her on the rescue mission. She had to figure on one meal, two at the most, and what she had placed in her flour-sack grub bag ought to be enough.

The street was quiet, deserted, but several of the saloons including the Marigold were still going strong as she made her way towards Englehart's Livery Stable, where she was to join Curly, Walt Crow and the kid, Tom Horn. They would have the horses saddled and ready, the plan being to ride out immediately, taking care not to be seen or heard, proceed to the buttes through which

Luke and the marshal, John Rye, would be passing, and there lay an ambush.

Curly and the others would do the shooting. They didn't like lawmen, particularly this John Rye, they claimed, who walked around giving everybody the impression that he was invincible and that the bullet hadn't been made that could cut him down. Curly said he was hoping to prove him wrong in that, so she was just leaving it up to him and the others to get Rye out of the way.

While she had tucked Luke's short-barreled pistol into a pocket of her baggy trousers, she figured there'd be no reason for using it—but she would and she could if it became necessary. She was taking no chances with John Rye. He was about as compassionate as a pack of starving wolves, someone had said, and that was exactly how she'd treat him—showing no consideration or mercy if it came down to that point.

She had to admit, however, that he appeared to be quite a man, and from the tales that had gone around ever since word got out that he was coming to town after Luke, he evidently was. Even the toughest of the hardcases had made themselves scarce, and while they perhaps weren't actually afraid of him, they preferred to avoid any confrontation.

He'd never lost a prisoner although he'd handled dozens of the worst kind, according to those who knew of him. Some never got to where he was taking them alive, that was true, but that was their own fault. You couldn't really blame them, Zoe guessed; they were men destined to hang once they arrived at their destination, anyway, so as well die one way as another.

That's the position Luke was in. He was a dead man if Rye got him to Yuma Prison, and that, she supposed, was the reason she felt obliged to help him. It wasn't that he meant anything to her anymore; that first soaring flush of what she'd thought was genuine love had withered within the first month of marriage, after which it had all become merely a matter of convenience and habit.

Luke had fooled her good and she was still finding it difficult to face up to that fact. Orphaned at fifteen by a party of renegade Kiowas who attacked the wagon train in which she and her parents were moving West, she had been on her own for years, working in saloons, restaurants and once for a time in a ladies dress shop, where the spinster proprietress had managed to instill some of the gentler graces of womanhood and a smattering of education within her.

But there was little money in that way of life and she'd returned to the more lucrative pastures of the saloons, more or less settling down at the age of twenty in the booming New Mexico Territory town of Las Vegas. There, in the Silver Dollar, the largest and most popular of several such establishments, she worked herself up to dealing faro and was doing right well when Luke Braden came into her life.

He walked in one bright day, all fine clothes, broad smile and a manner to him that sent tremors chasing up and down her backbone. She'd never met a man just like him and when he began to shower her with attention, all the while throwing gold eagles around like they were going out of style, her usual cynicism built up from bitter experience, simply melted away. Within two weeks' time they were married.

Disillusionment wasn't long in setting in. Luke proved to be a liar, shiftless, weak and an eye out for every woman that passed his way. The supply of eagles—the source of which she never did find out—was soon exhausted and supporting him became her lot.

Eventually, to get him out of a bad situation he'd fallen into, she quit her job at the Silver Dollar and they moved to Boston City. There the final blow fell when she learned he was a murderer with a hangman's rope waiting for him. He was clapped into jail to be held until John Rye, a Special U. S. Marshal, arrived to take charge of him.

She guessed she should have called it quits right then and there, marriage vows be damned. But somehow she couldn't force herself to do it. She'd made a bargain and was not the sort to back out of it simply because of her own bad judgment. She'd bailed Luke out of trouble before, only too often, and she'd have to do it again—or at least try. But it was different this time; never before had there been a man like John Rye to contend with.

But this was it—the wind-up. She'd told herself that the night before, that once he was out of this jam she was through with him—once and for all. She'd go her way and he damned well could go his.

Taking him away from John Rye wasn't going to be any Sunday sociable, and she could only wish she'd have better help when it came to making the effort. Curly Hyde, Walt Crow and Tom Horn—two shiftless saloon bums who fancied themselves tough, and a wet-eared kid.

But that was typical of Luke, of the kind he took up with. His friends couldn't have been some of the real hardcases like the Jennings bunch, who would pitch in and get a job done regardless of all else if they thought enough of a man; no, they had to be the likes of Horn and Walt Crow and that sneaky Curly.

It was a hell of note that she'd be depending on them —and not too comfortable, either. Curly and Walt were always whispering among themselves when she was around and they had a way of looking her over that made her feel she was being stripped naked. If ever she had to use the pistol in her pocket, or the little forty-one der- ringer she was wearing inside her boot, odds were it would be to protect herself from them.

But that was nothing new. She'd been fending off un- welcome hands with various degrees of success since the massacre, and marriage to Luke Braden hadn't changed anything. *"You're just too goddam pretty-looking for your own good,"* he'd once told her when she'd appealed to him for protection from an overly amorous drover. He'd only laughed it off and she'd been forced to hide out in one of the other girl's quarters to escape the big Texan.

That was the way it had been after that incident, she looking out for her own welfare as before. For a husband, Luke was nothing, a leech, a millstone around her neck— but she'd not get all worked up again hashing it about in her mind. She was on the way to ridding herself of him by freeing him from the law—and once that was done her sense of loyalty and obligation would be satisfied and she could resume a life of her own again.

Her steps slowed as she drew abreast of the jail. A dim

light glowed in the window; likely Rye or old Marshal Whitaker was in there keeping night watch over their prisoner. It could be Linus Kirby, too. He'd been taken in by Luke's charm, more or less, and could have asked for the duty.

Actually she doubted there was any need to guard Luke. Nobody in town really cared enough about him to try and break him out. Folks took him for what he was— a big smiler, a glad-handing four-flusher, and nothing else. He simply wouldn't be worth going up against the law for, particularly when the law was represented by a man like John Rye.

She moved on, hurrying a little now. Englehart's barn was only a short distance down the street and the sooner they got mounted, rode to the buttes and laid the ambush along the trail, the better she'd feel.

What would she do when it was all over? Where would she go? Denver, maybe. Things were booming up in that area, she'd been told, and with the mines giving up fortunes in silver and gold, she might hit it big. One thing for sure, she could not stay around Boston City—or even in the area; there'd be one hell of a hullabaloo spring up in the wake of Luke's rescue, especially if Curly or one of the others put a bullet in Rye's head.

"That you, Zoe?"

Hyde's voice reached out from the blackness of the livery stable. Her pace quickened even more. They were there, waiting and ready.

"It's me. We all set?"

Hyde, the scar-faced man stepped into the open. "Reckon we are," he drawled, "'ceptin we're too late."

"Too late!" she echoed, moving through the wide door-way and halting before the three men. "What's that mean?"

"Means just what it means—we're too late. That lawman rode out with Luke sometime last night—right after dark, we figure."

Anger rushed through the girl. "How do you know?"

"Well, the hostler said the marshal come got Luke's horse and gear along with that lawman's animal, and they was all fixed up for traveling. . . . They sure ain't here in the barn. We looked good."

"What about the jail?"

"Luke's cell's empty. You can see from the window. The marshal's sleeping in the chair."

Zoe Braden smiled tightly. Rye had tricked her. So be it, but the tune wasn't finished yet; there were still a few verses.

"Makes no difference," she snapped, crossing to the waiting horses standing in the runway. "Mount up. We can catch them."

"Yes'm," Hyde said in his satisfied voice. "We was all hoping that's how you'd feel about it."

5

Daybreak found John Rye and his prisoner across the state line and in the Territory of New Mexico. The lawman, hopeful of avoiding any problems with Zoe Braden and any other person harboring thoughts of aiding his charge to escape, had pressed the horses hard. Now, looking out over the broad, beautiful grassland rolling away endlessly before them in the pale amber glow of the rising sun, he realized they must soon halt and rest their mounts.

He glanced at Luke Braden. The outlaw was slumped on his black, eyes closed, muscles of his somewhat handsome features slack. He had complained throughout the night, first at departing upon the advent of darkness, then at being chained to the saddle, the lack of food, at being compelled to go by horseback rather than stagecoach, and at not being able to bid his wife farewell. All had fallen on deaf ears; the marshal, true to his customary self, had paid not the slightest attention to Braden's whinings.

Reaching a high roll in the trail, he twisted about, and, one hand braced against the cantle, the other on the horn, he studied their back trail carefully. After a time he came back around. They were not being followed—so far. If luck was with him and Rufe Whitaker was able to keep his deputy from leaking information, no one would have become aware of their absence until the morning; with such a lead it should be easy to keep well ahead of any-one with thoughts of helping the outlaw.

Off to his right Rye spotted a low swale in which sev-eral cottonwoods grew. He doubted there'd be a spring there but it didn't matter. He had filled both canteens back in Boston City, and since the night had been more than cool, they'd consumed only a small amount.

Swinging the chestnut gelding from the trail, and yank-ing on the rope connected to Braden's black, he angled down the slope to the coulee. They'd haul up there for an hour or so, make coffee and eat a little of the bread and dried meat he carried in his grub sack while the horses rested. With the night's start they had, the time could be spared.

Braden came to with a jerk as they drew to a halt be-neath the freshly leafed-out trees. Dismounting, Rye un-locked one of the steel cuffs that secured the outlaw to the saddle and unceremoniously pulled him off his horse. Shoving him roughly up to the nearest cottonwood, he pulled a six-foot length of chain, also equipped with cuffs, from his saddlebags, took a turn around the trunk of the tree with it and then fastened the metal circles about Braden's ankles.

"Ain't no sense in this!" the outlaw protested as Rye restored the loose wrist manacle to its place. "I ain't go-ing no place—not with you carrying a gun and just aching to shoot me. Besides, them leg irons are pinching."

"Get used to it," the marshal said indifferently, scrap-ing together bits of wood scattered about for a fire.

"That's the way it'll be from here on when we stop until you're locked in a Yuma Prison cell."

Braden swore raggedly. "Just ain't no reason—"

"One good one," Rye said bluntly, striking a match to the pile of wood. "Keeps me from worrying about you when my back's turned."

The outlaw, made a part of the sturdy tree by the encircling chain, manacled hands in his lap, fell silent as he watched the marshal set a can of water over the fire and dig into his grub sack for the food on which they would make a quick meal.

"Hell of a poor feed for a man," he grumbled a bit later, accepting a chunk of bread and a portion of the dried beef.

"It'll do until dark."

The water came to a boil and Rye, adding a handful of crushed coffee beans, set the blackened container aside, stirred down the rising froth with a twig. When the thick liquid had settled he filled two cups, handed one to Braden.

Luke took the tin without comment. An ease seemed to have come over him, a sort of confidence as if he believed the treatment he was receiving from the hard-nosed lawman was of a temporary nature and it was only wise to make the best of it.

Rye did not miss the change and if it troubled him to even the slightest degree he did not show it. The bread and meat finished, the strong black coffee drunk, he returned the utensils to their containers and rose. Taking one of the canteens, he crossed to where the horses were grazing on sweet grama, and, soaking his bandanna, squeezed out a cupful or so into the animals' mouths. That done, he retraced his steps to the camp and, selecting a level place, stretched out, hat cocked over his eyes to shield them from the climbing sun.

Rye awoke promptly an hour later. Sitting up, he glanced at Braden. The outlaw, knees drawn up, was staring at him, eyes filled with sly amusement. The lawman smiled in his grim, knowing way and got to his feet.

"Don't bet on it," he said, reading Braden's mind.

It was a situation he'd been through half a hundred times. Prisoners were always confident of escape by one means or another—many of them right up to the moment they were pushed through the door of a cell.

"Don't bet on what?" Luke demanded indignantly. His expression had altered quickly.

"On somebody—maybe your wife—taking you away from me. It won't happen."

The outlaw's eyes spread with surprise. Evidently he was unaware that Zoe had made known her intentions. His mouth tightened, and then he shrugged.

"Maybe," he muttered.

Rye, moving away from him, ignored the comment. He wanted another look at the country behind them, taking no chances on simply assuming they were not being pursued. He had learned long ago that it was foolhardy, and could easily be fatal, to take things for granted.

The wide horizon to the north was empty. A half dozen buzzards soaring in the bright, spotless blue of the sky overhead and activity in a village of fat prairie dogs off to his right were the only signs of life to be seen.

He stood for a time, his narrowed glance drifting over

the land, noting the splashes of vivid color where wild flowers had broken into early blossom, the long, graceful slopes of emerald green grass, the lighter gray shade of the sage. Here and there other small groves of cottonwoods showed their pale color to the sun and on the crests and slopes of choppy hills cedars, bayonet yucca, thistle and beds of prickly-pear cactus were making their stand.

It was a fine country, he thought, one ideal for raising cattle but not, as the hopeful immigrants who had been persuaded to part with their hard-earned cash for land around Boston City had been led to believe, suitable for farming.

He turned away, put his attention to the south and west. They would bear in that general direction, pointing for the Canadian River. There was a well-defined trail that led to the town of Cimarron, but it would be wise to avoid it. If no one saw him en route with his prisoner, then no one could tell of their passing.

He would have to stop at Cimarron, however. They needed to take on the few supplies he had intentionally avoided buying in Boston City—coffee, bacon, salt, several other items. Once restocked he shouldn't have to bother entering a town again until they were well into Arizona, and that pleased him. It was always a good plan to stay clear of the settlements, just as it was smart to avoid trains and stagecoaches when transporting a prisoner. Alone and away from other men it was much easier to keep matters under control.

Cimarron couldn't be much more than a half day's ride ahead, he reckoned, if he wanted to push the horses. But such wasn't necessary. He'd take it at a steady but not fast pace, save the animals. The need might arise to call on them for speed and he didn't want them tired.

Dropping back to the camp, he walked by the seemingly dozing Braden to the horses. Tightening the cinches, he led them to where the outlaw sprawled. Rousing him, he unlocked the leg chains, returned them to his saddlebags, and, assisting Luke onto his black, secured his hands to the fork once again by running the short chain connecting the cuffs through its opening.

"Ain't right, making me ride like this," the outlaw complained sullenly. "Damn near kills me, way my shoulders and back ache."

"Like everything else, you'll get used to it," Rye said, swinging up onto the chestnut. "Time we reach Yuma you won't be noticing it."

"Goddam you!" Braden shouted in a sudden explosion of anger. "If I ever get a chance I'll—"

"You won't," the lawman cut in calmly, and taking up the black's lead rope, moved out from under the cottonwoods.

6

It was well past midafternoon when Cimarron came into view. It had taken somewhat longer than Rye had anticipated, but he had not pressed the tired horses and there had been numerous halts to rest them. The many hours were telling on both men, also, particularly Braden.

"Bed's sure going to feel good," he said wearily as they drew near a small grove to the east of the settlement. "Saddle's about growed to my—"

"We'll be camping farther on—"

"Camp!" Luke echoed in an exasperated voice. "There's a good hotel in this town. Why can't we put up there?"

"Stay clear of towns—it's a rule of mine," Rye said shortly.

He could have gone further into it, explained that to do so quite often caused trouble. People asked questions; occasionally the prisoner would have a friend turn up who took it upon himself to render aid—and there were always the bleeding hearts who felt sorry for a shackled man, but he let it drop.

"These goddam rules of yours," Braden moaned. "I just don't see why."

"You don't need to," the lawman snapped, halting well back in the trees. "I'll be leaving you here while I ride in.

Few things I need to buy, and my horse's got a loose shoe."

Dismounting, he unlocked one of Braden's cuffs, allowed him to leave the saddle. Returning the manacle to the outlaw's wrist, he then obtained the leg chain and, pushing the man up to a tall, lightning-scarred stump, he attached him to it as before with the cottonwood.

Braden, protesting, muttering curses all the while, slumped against the blackened tree trunk. "Treating me like I was a dog—"

Rye, picketing the outlaw's horse a short distance away, smiled blandly, and, crossing to his chestnut, climbed into the saddle. Taking a final look around, reassuring himself that he was leaving the outlaw far enough from the trail where he would neither be seen nor heard, he cut back through the stand of trees and rode a short distance to the settlement.

Cimarron, the center of an area healing slowly from a long and bloody range war, lay near deserted in the afternoon sunlight as he turned into the main street. Two soldiers, probably from Fort Union, lounged in front of Lambert's Saloon; a woman and a small boy were coming out of the general store, and some distance on down the twin row of buildings a man was washing the front windows of his establishment. Glancing about, Rye located the blacksmith shop and pointed the gelding toward it.

The smith, a large, dark man with close-cropped hair, was dozing on a wagon seat set against one wall of his open shed as the lawman rode in. He came to his feet lazily, and, taking a leather apron from a peg, ambled forward.

"Something I can do for you?" he asked, surveying Rye critically.

"Horse of mine's losing a shoe. Left hind leg. Can you take care of it right away?"

The smith nodded. "Reckon so, seeing as how I ain't doing nothing."

Rye handed the chestnut's reins to the man. "Thirty minutes—that give you enough time?"

"Won't take no more'n that, for sure."

The marshal wheeled away, doubling back to Lambert's. Nodding to the two soldiers as he strode by them, he entered the low-ceilinged, thick-walled structure and stepped up to the bar. There were several more blue-uniformed men lolling about along with a number of civilian patrons.

"Whiskey," he said as the bartender paused expectantly in front of him.

The man turned, obtained a glass and, placing it before Rye, took up a half-empty bottle on the counter. And then, as if having second thoughts, he abandoned it, reached down to a lower shelf hidden from view and produced a bottle bearing a distillery label.

Filling the lawman's glass, he said, "Be two bits."

Rye laid a silver dollar on the counter. The bartender, making change from a small tin box, returned the coins and watched the marshal down his drink.

"Best in the house," he said, smiling.

Rye nodded in agreement, pushed the glass forward

for a refill. It was good, bonded liquor, a treat when compared to the usual rotgut obtainable in most saloons.

"Man don't come across whiskey like that often."

"Boss got to stocking it for a special customer that used to come in," the bartender said. "Name was Allison. Moved away—to Texas, I been told." He paused, looked closely at Rye. "You happen to know him?"

Clay Allison . . . One of the leaders in the range war. A hero to some, and outlaw to others.

"Heard the name mentioned," the marshal said, noncommittally.

"Was big shucks around here for a spell," the man behind the counter said, again studying Rye. "I know you?"

"Doubt it," the lawman replied, taking up his refilled glass.

"Sure something familiar about you. Maybe it was a picture or—"

"How about some of that good stuff down here, Frank?" a patron at the opposite end of the counter broke in.

Wrapping a big hand around the labeled bottle, the barkeep moved off to satisfy his customer. Rye, sipping at the bourbon, came about, leaned against the counter and let his flat glance drift over the room. From a table against the wall two soldiers eyed him narrowly. Recognizing instantly the signs of trouble, he started to turn away. Immediately the pair arose, moved unsteadily toward him.

Rye tossed off the remainder of his drink, set the glass back on the counter. Somewhere out in the street a man was yelling to someone farther down in the town and off in the direction of the livery stable a jackass brayed.

"I got you pegged!" the shorter of the two soldiers, a corporal, said thickly, lurching into the lawman.

Rye pulled aside, nodded coldly as conversation in the saloon came to a stop. Few things irritated him so much as a quarrelsome drunk, and he was now faced with a couple of them.

"Seen you bring in one of our boys. Deserter, he was— when I was at Fort Lyon."

Rye remained silent. He had no recollection of the occasion but there had been a few times when he'd been called on to deliver an army prisoner.

"Ain't got no use for a deserter," the corporal declared, speaking loud enough for all in the saloon to hear, "but the shape that private was in when this jasper showed up with him was something pitiful . . . Yessir, pitiful!"

"Now I know who you are!" the bartender shouted abruptly, his round face lighting up. "You're that U. S. Marshal they call the—"

"Never mind," Rye cut in sharply, and, taking his change, started for the door.

The corporal rocked forward. Grabbing Rye by the arm, he said, "Now, hold on just a goddam minute, you—"

The marshal's hand swept down, came up fast. Lamplight glinted on metal as the pistol he held arced through the smoky air, landed solidly against the side of the soldier's head. Instantly the remaining uniformed men in the room leaped to their feet, surged toward him.

The lawman faced them coolly, gun hanging loosely

in his fingers. Eyes glazed, mouth gaped, the corporal had sagged into the arms of his friend.

"Back off," Rye said in a quiet, level voice. "You'd be fools to get shot up over a drunk."

"Ain't nobody jumps one of us and gets away with it," a thick-necked buck sergeant muttered, pushing out a step in front of the others. "Mister, whoever you are, you've made a mistake."

"It'll be you making the mistake," Rye replied softly. "And far as me jumping him, it was the other way around. Now, I'm walking out of here. I'll kill any of you that follows me. It's that simple."

Holstering his weapon, the marshal pulled away from the bar and crossed to the door. Behind him the saloon lay in total silence, and then as he stepped out into the open, a harsh voice broke the hush.

"There'll come another time—"

John Rye halted, pivoted slowly. His features were wooden and for the first time there was a hard glint in his eyes.

"What about now?" he asked, carefully spacing his words. "Here in the street—be as good a place as any."

Silent then, the lawman rode out the tension-filled moments that followed his invitation. There was no response. Wheeling again, he moved on, crossed to the general store. When he reached the steps leading up to the landing, he glanced back. No one had emerged from Lambert's; only the two soldiers now leaning against the saloon's hitchrack were to be seen.

Shrugging, Rye entered the store. Everybody had friends, for one reason or another, and the incident had been no unusual experience, but it had been his hope to transact his business and pass on unnoticed, thus leaving no trace of his whereabouts for Zoe Braden and Luke's friends, if they were following, to uncover. The reverse had been the case. He had drawn attention to himself and the advantages of anonymity were now lost.

Obtaining the supplies needed from the merchant, he returned to the street and made his way to the black-smith's shop. The chestnut was ready, and, paying the half-dollar fee stated, he mounted and loped back to the grove where he had staked out Luke Braden.

Caution was second nature to John Rye, and before he came in sight of the outlaw, he veered to the east, made his approach from a different direction; there was always that chance some passing rider, or party of riders, could stumble onto a cached prisoner, and, sympathizing with him, take steps to set him free. Strangely enough a law-man's lot all too often was that of a villain and misplaced compassion was seldom in short supply.

Halting deep in the grove, Rye sat for a full five minutes watching Braden and listening for sounds that would indicate the presence of others. Finally convinced the out-law was alone, he rode in. Braden met him with an angry stare.

"About time you was coming back! Ain't human, treat-ing me like this, and by God, I ain't going to stand for it!"

Rye merely smiled, added the supplies to his grub sack, and then, releasing Braden, got him back onto the saddle and secured to its fork. Climbing slowly back onto the weary chestnut, he took up the black's lead rope and worked through the trees into the open. Pausing, he glanced toward Cimarron. There was no sign of anyone coming from the settlement. The soldiers had apparently elected to let their indignation over his treatment of their corporal end there in the saloon. He shifted his attention then to the north. A hardness came into his features.

Four riders . . . They were not on the trail; instead, they were well off to the side, which could only mean they were following tracks—tracks left by his chestnut and the black Luke Braden was riding. . . . Zoe and the outlaw's three friends.

7

Luke Braden also noted the oncoming riders. At once a triumphant grin spread across his face as he jerked his head in their direction.

"Knowed they'd be coming after me! Told you so, didn't I? Now, Mister Lawman, you'd best start thinking about what you ought to do—and that's turn me loose. They's four of them to your one. Sure can't beat them odds!"

"Maybe," Rye said indifferently, placing his attention on the country to the west. "You'd be smart to do a little figuring yourself. They could get you killed trying to take you away from me."

Braden frowned, sobered. "You saying you'll shoot me before you'll let them do it?"

"What it'll amount to. You're a dead man anyway. What difference does it make if it happens here or in Yuma Prison? Dead's dead."

Braden stared at Rye in disbelief. "Hell, you can't do that! You're the law. Up to you to keep a prisoner alive, not shoot him down. I got rights—"

"Not far as I'm concerned," Rye said callously. "Let's go."

Raking the chestnut with his spurs, the marshal put the big horse to a lazy lope, trailing Braden's reluctant mount behind him. There appeared to be broken country five miles or so in the distance, and with darkness coming on, he should have no trouble in locating a good hideout for the night. With the horses in such worn condition, he could not hope to continue much farther.

"Ain't no use running," Braden said, his voice again confident. "They'll catch up and once they do it'll be the boneyard for you. That's my woman bringing some of my friends, and there ain't none of them going to quit 'til I'm free."

The lawman, turning his head now and then to check on Zoe Braden and the men with her, seemed not to hear. That he and his prisoner had been spotted shortly after they broke out of the grove was evident since the party had abandoned the course they were following, were now slicing diagonally across a wide flat in hopes of effecting an interception.

There was small possibility they could pull it off. Their mounts had covered the same distance as the black and the chestnut, would be no less tired, and the ragged buttes area was steadily drawing nearer.

"Horse of mine's going to cave in if'n we don't stop!" Braden warned.

The marshal glanced over his shoulder. The black was showing signs of buckling. "Keep his head up!" he ordered. "Be stopping in a mile or so. You let him fall and you'll find yourself running alongside me the rest of the way."

Luke swore. "By God—I'll bet you'd do that—"

"Count on it," Rye said, and threw his attention again to the north.

The riders had gained slightly. He could make them out now; Zoe Braden, in a man's clothing, was slightly ahead of the others. He strained to get a better look at their features. One was Curly Hyde, the kid they called Tom Horn was next to him. On the far left was the scar-faced Crow. They were the same three Rufe Whitaker had pointed out to him that day before at the jail.

Knowing who they were helped some. Not one of them appeared to be anything more than barflies and bums and could be expected to back off fast if it came to a showdown. But that wasn't always the way it worked out, and any kind of a man could shoot from the dark or put a bullet in another's back; it took little if any charac-ter to pull a trigger.

The rim of the badlands loomed ahead, a dark, ragged edge. It was mostly a broad sink, Rye saw as he viewed it in the slanting sunlight—a wild area of buttes, arroyos and littered with high brush and rocks. Stunted cedars appeared to be the only trees and he realized at once that a suitable hiding place would not be as easily found as he'd thought.

The trail dipped sharply off the flat and the horses slowed as they began the steep descent. Rye flung a final look at Zoe Braden and the men accompanying her. They were less than a half mile in the distance; he would have to act quickly.

Reaching the foot of the embankment and again on fairly level ground, he roweled the chestnut, urging him into a weary trot. A hundred yards or so on ahead a spur of dense brush pushed out from one side of the sink while the trail continued to wind its way on beyond it over the gravelly floor in an opposite direction. If they could gain the heavy growth in time, the chances for getting Zoe and her party off his back would be better than good.

Again he spurred the flagging chestnut, jerked hard on the lead rope attached to Braden's black.

"They got you right where they want you, Marshal," the outlaw called cheerfully. "Next thing you'll be hearing will be them opening up on you from somewheres above."

They reached the edge of the brush. Rye swerved the gelding into it, still using his spurs savagely. The big red horse plunged into the depths of the buckthorn and other rank shrubbery, dragging the failing black with him, Braden cursing steadily all the while.

"You ain't going to ditch them in here!"

Rye pulled to a stop behind an outsized boulder in the center of the dense thicket. He was off his horse instantly and at the outlaw's side in two long steps. Key in hand, he released one of Braden's cuffs, and, pulling him from the saddle, threw him to the ground. Crouched over the outlaw, pistol poised, he nodded coldly.

"One sound and I'll bust in your skull."

Braden swallowed noisily. "Sure—sure—"

The rattle of displaced gravel at the edge of the sink shattered the late afternoon hush. Somewhere nearby an insect, stilled by the approach of the chestnut and the black, resumed its raucous clacking, and back in the direction of Cimarron a cow lowed anxiously.

The clatter increased. All four of the riders were now descending the path; Rye guessed they would shortly reach the trail below. Taut, he waited, listened, sweat shining on his forehead. The dull thump of hooves beyond the spur of brush reached him. Zoe and the others were sticking to the trail, well marked by riders in the past.

"Can't see them no more—"

It was the voice of one of the men, just which, Rye had no way of knowing.

"They're on ahead of us," Zoe Braden replied. "Have to be. No place to go but straight on."

"Reckon you're right. Just all that brush and rocks are hiding them. They'll be getting out of here farther on. We'll be seeing them again then."

The voices were gradually fading and he could no longer hear the thud of hooves. Rye did not stir. Finally, when there was no doubt the party was well beyond the end of the thicket, he drew himself upright and ordered Braden again onto the saddle. As he chained him to the fork once more the outlaw wagged his head wearily. All the cocksure confidence was gone from his voice.

"Ain't we camping here? Hell—I'm plumb beat out, can't go no farther."

"We're doubling back, getting up on the flat," Rye said. "Be a place along there where we can stop."

"Horse of mine'll never make it."

"He'll make it, all right," the lawman said in a promising sort of way. "You'll see to it."

8

"This here's far as we're going—sugar," Walt Crow said as they halted at the end of the sink and looked out over a broad, starlit flat. "Me and the boys're plumb tuckered and these here nags are ready to fall down."

Zoe, too weary to resent the scar-faced man's familiarity, shrugged hopelessly. They had followed the rough trail through the brush-filled basin until it climbed once more to lay its trace across the vast mesa—and caught no sight of Luke and his lawman captor.

Had she made a mistake? The possibility of such was beginning to grow in her mind. John Rye just may have tricked her; he could have led her to believe he was ahead, but had pulled off somewhere in the closing darkness, and, hiding in the dense brush, allowed her to ride by. Then, when there was no danger of being seen or heard, he could have doubled back and taken another trail—one, perhaps, that skirted the sink.

There was no way of knowing for sure until daylight, at which time they could look for tracks. Curly Hyde was an expert at such, and if he found no prints leading up out of the basin to the flat, she'd know for certain Rye had fooled her.

She would have to decide then what must be done, backtrack and search out the new route taken by the lawman and Luke, or gamble, strike a course due east across open country and hope to intercept them. The former would consume valuable time, throw her at least a day, possibly more, behind Rye, and the success of her plan depended upon getting in front of him and setting up an ambush.

"You hear me, pretty lady?"

Crow's persistence angered her. "That'll be enough of that kind of talk!" she flared, whirling to him. Then, in a less irritated voice, she added: "All right, we'll camp here."

Cutting the little buckskin she was riding about, she dropped back into the sink, and, halting beside a squat cedar, dismounted. The men following silently, drew up a few paces beyond.

Behind her the wall of the deep wash rose to shoulder height above the sandy floor. It would serve well as a shield against the chill wind that would ride in the early morning hours to sweep across the flats from the towering Sangre de Cristo Mountains to the west. There was ample firewood available, and while there was neither water nor an abundance of grass for the horses, they would get by. All in all, she thought, it wasn't a bad place to lay over for the night.

Except that she wasn't particularly prepared. The food she'd brought along was already depleted, their noon meal having made deep inroads on the amount. She simply hadn't figured on being on the trail for this long. Damn that John Rye! If he'd done as he'd said he would, it would all be over now and she'd be back in Boston City or on her way to some other town.

But Rye—damn him again—had crossed her up. And now here she was, miles from nowhere, with practically no food and three saloon bums she'd probably have to use her pistol on before the night was over, while Luke, the reason for it all, was somewhere miles away.

Simmering, Zoe slipped the buckskin's bridle, neck-roped him to the cedar, and began to loosen the saddle cinch. Immediately she heard someone move up through the darkness, stop beside her.

"Ain't no use of you doing that—not when you got me around," Crow said in a low voice.

"Look after your own horse," the girl replied. "I can manage."

"Just wanting to help you—"

"I don't need any help—and if you're looking for something to do, get a fire started so I can make coffee."

"Sure, honey," Walt Crow murmured, and faded off into the night.

Zoe remained motionless beside the buckskin for a long minute, and then, lifting the saddle, she swung it off the worn horse and set it on a nearby clump of rabbit bush. Tired as she was, the leather hull was almost more than she could handle, but she knew it was a chore that must be done by her; to relent the slightest in her attitude toward the three men would lead to trouble.

Taking up her saddlebags, she crossed to the fire Crow had under way and which was now beginning to spread a warm light into the darkness. She could see Horn and Curly Hyde beyond the flare, working with their horses. Crow was hunched beside the flames, cracking dry limbs with his big, thick-fingered hands and piling them where they would be convenient.

He glanced up as she drew near, grinned broadly. "Here's your fire. All we're needing is something to cook on it."

The girl shook her head. "Coffee, that's about it. There's a little of the bread and meat left that we can divide up."

Digging into the leather pouches, she produced the granite pot she'd brought along, passed it to Walt. He reached for a canteen hanging from a bush, pulled the cork with his teeth and, filling the container, placed it over the flames.

"Going to get mighty cold tonight," he said. "Reckon we'd best keep this fire going."

Ignoring the comment, Zoe continued to dig about in the saddlebags for the remainder of her food supply, the sack of coffee and the cups with which to drink. Hyde and Tom Horn came up at that moment, their chores completed, and hunched beside Crow. The older of the two had a bottle of whiskey in his hand and, leaning forward, he offered it to Walt.

"Have a snort of this here red-eye. Sort of takes the chill out of a man, loosens him up a mite."

Crow grinned, and taking the bottle started to raise it to his lips. He paused, thrust it at Zoe. "Sure forgetting my manners. Ladies ought to be first."

"No thanks," Zoe said, and, using the saddlebags as a table, placed the scraps of bread and meat on them. "Here's all we've got left. Split it between you. Soon as the water's hot there'll be coffee."

Crow, taking a swallow of the liquor, raised his thick brows. "Ain't you eating nothing?"

"I'm not hungry," the woman answered, and moved back to where she could rest against her saddle.

The night's cold was setting in and, drawing her jacket closer, she pulled the folded blanket used on the buckskin from beneath the hull and shook it out. She had not come prepared for the night, either, and therefore had no bedroll. But the wool cover used with the saddle would be enough, particularly if she slept near the fire.

Draping the blanket about her shoulders, Zoe returned to where the men were. The water in the pot had come to a boil and one of them had added the coffee. Crow was now filling the cups, all of which, she noted, already contained a liberal portion of Hyde's whiskey.

Picking up the one set aside for her, she tossed the liquor into the brush and refilled the tin container with coffee. Crow and Hyde watched her with sly amusement while Horn looked on, seemingly out of it insofar as they were concerned. Being much younger, they ignored him most of the time.

"Shouldn't've done that, lady," Walt Crow said, wagging his head. "Little red-eye'll warm you up."

"Coffee will do for me," Zoe said, coolly. "Tomorrow we'll have to get supplies from somewhere."

"Cimarron, that's the closest town," Hyde said. "We can cut back to there."

"Cut back—that mean we've already passed it?"

"Yep. It's sort of east and north of us now."

"There another town on ahead? I don't like the idea of doubling back. We'll lose too much ground."

"Could be," Crow said, coming into the discussion. "We don't know which way that tin star took Luke, however. Could be he's back in Cimarron right now, a-bellying up to a bar or maybe sleeping warm and nice in the hotel."

Zoe Braden doubted that. Rye didn't strike her as one who would be tempted by any such luxuries; being strictly all business, he was more likely to be camped out in some remote area far from other men who might be a source of trouble where his prisoner was concerned.

"Well, if you want my advice," Curly said, taking another pull at his bottle, "we'll just keep going. Trails all sort of run together on down near Vegas. We're bound to come across Luke and that marshal along there somewheres."

"I think that's the best thing to do," Zoe agreed. "But what about supplies?"

"Aw, we can shoot us a rabbit now and then, maybe. Besides, we'll be coming to some sodbuster's place or a ranch where we can get us a bite of grub. Might even be a town out there."

"Why can't one of us go back to Cimarron and get what we need?" Tom Horn wondered.

Crow glanced at Curly Hyde. "Now, that's a right smart idea!"

"Sure is, Tom. You could light out first thing in the morning. Won't take you long to get there, and if you move right along you ought to catch up to us about dark."

Zoe frowned, not too convinced of the merits of such a plan. But it was a good thought. They would have to get food somewhere, and depending on finding it along the trail could be risky; settlers, much less towns, in that wild, wide country were few and far between. Considering it, she reckoned she didn't have much choice.

"What do you think, lady?" Crow asked. "For my part, I say we ought to do it."

"All right, Tom," she said, nodding to the younger man. "I'll give you some money in the morning, and tell you what we need."

A reluctance seemed to have come over Horn. It was as if he regretted making the suggestion.

"How'll I know where to find you all?"

"You just head south out of Cimarron," Hyde said. "You'll spot us somewhere along the way."

"Can maybe even pick yourself up a partner if you want," Walt Crow said. "More'n likely you'll run into that deputy around there somewheres."

"Linus Kirby?" Zoe's voice was filled with surprise.

"Yes'm. Seems that marshal sort of slapped him pretty good over something. Might've been just whiskey talk he was doing there in the Marigold Saloon last night, but he claimed he was going after Rye and have it out with him."

"Do you think he meant it?"

"Sure, he meant it!" Hyde said. "Heard him tell he aimed to follow that marshal clean to Yuma Prison if he had to."

"I wish I'd known," Zoe murmured. "He could've come with us. We could use another good hand . . . Why didn't you say something to me about it?"

Walt Crow shrugged. "You told us to keep shut about

what we figured to do. Anyways, me and Curly are all the men you'll be needing. And the kid, here."

The girl sighed, sipped at her coffee. Back towards the mountains a coyote, or perhaps it was a wolf—she'd never learned to tell the difference—howled into the moonlight.

"You want the kid to go to Cimarron, that it?" Crow asked, as if anxious to be certain it was settled.

She nodded, her thoughts still on Linus Kirby. "I didn't know he'd had trouble with Rye—the deputy, I mean."

"That marshal's the kind that has trouble with everybody. You can always tell where he's been just from all the people he leaves hating him."

"I expect it's the only way he can do his job," Zoe said, and was immediately conscious that it sounded as if she were defending the lawman.

Curly Hyde laughed, helped himself to another drink. Crow tossed more wood onto the lowering fire while Tom Horn continued to stare into the flames, uncertainty still in his eyes. Somewhere below them in the sink an owl hooted, the mournful call seeming to hang in the deep hush. Zoe shivered, and, setting her cup down, drew the horse blanket closer to her body.

"I'll sleep on this side of the fire," she said, settling back, "expect you three to stay on the other."

Walt Crow grinned. "Whatever you want, lady."

"That's exactly what I want," Zoe said firmly, and, drawing the pistol from her pocket, laid it in her lap. "I'll keep this handy—just in case any of you forget."

9

On the first day out of the camp made on the Cimarron Flats, they reached the settlement of Vermillion, and Rye, following his usual custom, bypassed it with his prisoner at a considerable distance.

He pursued the same procedure, deaf to the complaints of Luke Braden, and avoided in the subsequent days, the towns of San Cristobal, Las Vegas and Vickston, where they cut due west toward a gap in a range of high mountains, and Albuquerque, where they crossed the wide, swiftly flowing Rio Grande.

Camping that night, after the fording, in a grove along the stream, they pushed on at first light, bearing steadily south and avoiding several small villages along the way.

They had made good time and John Rye was satisfied as he went through the customary procedure that evening of the fifth day of chaining his prisoner to one of the large cottonwoods that flourished throughout the length of the lush valley down which they were traveling. The going had been easy and there'd been no further signs of Zoe Braden and the men she'd enlisted to aid her.

He'd shaken her back in the sink, apparently, sent her on a useless chase and the chances were good she'd given up at that point. But true to his nature, the lawman could not fully accept such a conclusion until he was certain, and so occasionally paused to study their back trail for riders.

Socorro, one of the larger settlements in the territory, lay not far ahead, but it, too, would not bear witness to their passage. That fact, mentioned by him later as he and Braden suppered on the stew he'd prepared, brought the usual immediate storm of protests and complaints from the outlaw.

"Ain't no sense in it! You ain't going to get rid of Zoe—and we just as well be sleeping and eating where we'd be comfortable."

"You seen her lately?" Rye asked dryly.

"Nope, but that don't mean nothing. Everybody knows the road heading west out of Socorro is the only one leading to Arizona that's safe to use, and Zoe and the boys'll be riding straight for it."

"Could be," the lawman murmured.

"Ain't no doubt about it! Besides, Zoe's got Curly Hyde with her, and he's one hell of a good tracker. You sure ain't going to ever lose him. Giving them the slip back there at that sink just throwed them a day behind us."

"A day's all I want," Rye said.

Luke studied him in the pale orange flare of the fire. "You ain't anxious to tangle with her, are you, Mister Lawman? Well, can't say as I blame you. She's got notions all her—"

"Never killed a woman, just don't want to have to now," Rye cut in bluntly.

Braden's shoulders stirred. "Don't reckon she'll ever

give you the chance. She's a smart one, that Zoe, and she's got more guts than a army mule—"

"Too bad you didn't appreciate her more. Woman like that deserves something better than you."

"The hell! Kept her satisfied, didn't I? Plenty happy, too, I expect. If I hadn't, she wouldn't be out there now following me, figuring out a way to put a bullet in your head and get me loose."

"If she's out there—and I wouldn't lay any odds on it."

"She's there, sure enough. She ain't the quitting kind, and she'll dog your tracks 'til she gets the job done. I mean a-plenty to her."

"Could be she's doing it for a different reason."

Braden set his empty plate on a nearby rock, reached for his cup of coffee. "What other reason you talking about?"

"A woman takes her marriage vows serious, at least all the ones I've ever known do. She could be doing it—standing by you, they call it—just because you're her husband, not because you mean something to her."

"Naw, that ain't it," Braden said, pulling at his leg chain to change position. "If it was that, she'd a walked out on me a long time ago."

"Maybe she didn't—for the same reason."

The outlaw gave that a thought, wagged his head. He'd not shaved since that last morning in Boston City and a mat of dark whiskers now covered his cheeks and chin and the once neatly trimmed mustache had become a thick, ragged bit of brush.

"Don't make no sense to me," he muttered.

Rye refilled his cup and that of the outlaw with the

coffee. "Well, if it doesn't, there's no use of me trying to explain."

Draining the tin container, the lawman rose, walked to where the horses were grazing. They had fared well since reaching the Rio Grande Valley. Grass was plentiful and water for them was no problem. That would all change, however, once they were beyond Silver City on to the west, and angling across the lower part of Arizona Territory.

Taking the picket ropes, he led the animals to the edge of the river, and, finding a comfortable hummock upon which to sit, allowed them to drink their fill. His thoughts went again to Zoe Braden, and the hope that she had forsaken her intention to free Luke once more occupied his mind.

If she were still trailing them she would soon put in an appearance. Riding free and unencumbered she and the men with her could make much better time than could he with his prisoner. The day's lead he had on her could dissolve quickly, and, as Luke had pointed out, she would know the route he would be taking and be riding on a direct line for Socorro.

A hardness came into his face as he visualized the prospects. To him she must be considered nothing more or less than a threat, no different from a man seeking to accomplish the same purpose; and he would have to look upon her in the same light—kill her just as he would a man. He had a job to do, and do it he would, regardless.

Ordinarily he gave such possibilities no consideration. He had a sworn duty and in his line of work, dealing with the worst sort of criminals and their equally lawless friends, he had no compunction when it came to using his gun. As for her being a woman, well, that was the price she would have to pay for taking on a man's chore.

She should figure on being treated as one, bear the same risks, take the same chances. He couldn't be expected to make any allowances. There was no room in his way of life for such.

They were in the saddle and on the move at the usual early hour with Braden grumbling and cursing as always. Rye, his usual close-mouthed self, paid no heed, simply rode on, his features, in the pale glare lighting the east, taking on a bronzed, solid look while his whiskers appeared a glossy black.

The smoke of Socorro began to smudge the cloud-flecked sky to the south of them and shortly he swung out of the valley, veering more to his right, passing above a mass of barren rock which Mexican brigands once found convenient for their operations, and slanting toward higher, pine-clad hills on to the west. The main trail now lay well below them; they would stick to the rougher paths paralleling it and thus, as always, avoid any pilgrims on the move.

"Why don't we get on the road?" Braden demanded. "You're in such a goddamned hurry—we could move faster if we tried."

As before, John Rye allowed the outlaw's griping to fall unheeded. He had been through it all before, many times, and such was all in the day's work. Regardless of what was said, he would continue to follow a plan that experience had taught him was best—and the surest. No amount of objection or complaints would ever change him.

"Reckon we're going to have company, anyway," Luke

Braden said a time later as they topped out a rise and began to drop into a long valley.

The lawman had already noticed the five riders moving toward them from their left. He considered them in icy silence, suspicion at such times always a predominant factor in his thinking. Why would the men trouble to leave the main road, cut across country to intercept them?

Shifting on the saddle, he moved the holstered pistol on his hip forward to where it would be more readily available, and glanced at Braden. Luke had lapsed into silence, was watching the riders approach through eyes squinted to cut down the glare.

"Friends of yours?" the lawman asked.

The outlaw's mouth pulled into a tight grin. "Maybe."

Rye's hand dropped to the stock of the shotgun riding in the saddle boot. Drawing it, he laid it across his knees, both hammers at full cock.

"One wrong move," he said quietly, "and you're the first man dead."

Braden did not answer but the skin of his face had paled and a wildness had come into his eyes. The men drew nearer. Rye stiffened as he caught the glint of metal in the hand of the one in the lead. Abruptly a gunshot broke the warm stillness. Braden flinched as a bullet struck his saddle, screamed off into space. Instantly John Rye swung the shotgun around.

"Run for it!" he shouted at the outlaw, and fired both barrels of the heavy-gauge directly at the riders now spurring toward them.

10

"It's the kid—"

At Walt Crow's words Zoe glanced over her shoulder. A rider was approaching from the north. It was the second day after Tom Horn had been dispatched to Cimarron for supplies, and she had all but given up on his returning. They hadn't gone hungry, however; a homesteader had parted with a small amount of food from his meager store when she'd offered him a dollar, and that supplemented by a rabbit shot by Hyde had gotten them by.

In an effort to gain as much as possible on Rye, Zoe had cut directly across country, avoiding the easier, more circuitous established routes that would have taken them by the settlements. The marshal, she knew, would have wasted no time visiting towns along the way and it was only smart she follow his example. But the hour had been near when they would be forced to seek out a settlement and lay in supplies. Albuquerque, where they would be crossing the Rio Grande, would be a logical place, both Hyde and Crow had agreed; it lay only a day ahead. Now, with Horn's arrival, the halt there would not be necessary.

Pulling up beside a high rock ledge at the mouth of a narrow canyon they were entering, she wheeled about.

Curly and Crow, sullen and uncommunicative throughout the day after failing to break down her pistol-reinforced resistance the night before, drew up a few paces below, their features dark and showing no pleasure at the boy's appearance.

"Mighty sorry it took me so long," Horn said, riding past the two men and halting before her. "Had me a hard time finding you." Reaching back, he took two well-filled flour sacks tied together saddlebag fashion and hung across the skirt of his hull, and passed them to her.

"Everything you was wanting is there—"

"Thank you, Tom," Zoe said, slinging the sacks across her own saddle. "This will save us a lot of time."

Horn nodded, looked at the two men studying him with expressionless faces. "Yes'm, it sure will . . . Howdy, Curly, Walt."

Crow's tight lips cracked into a grin. "Howdy, yourself, kid. We're sure glad to see you—was beginning to worry a mite, thinking maybe you'd got yourself in a peck of trouble or something."

"Nothing like that," Horn said. "It was your telling me to keep heading south out of Cimarron. You're plenty to the west."

Curly shrugged. "We figured you'd have sense enough to know we'd be sort of going slanchways."

Zoe, unwilling to lose even a few minutes, and finished with securing the supplies to her saddle, motioned to the men and moved out, riding side by side up a wide, sandy-floored arroyo that led into the canyon.

"You bump into the deputy anywhere along the way?" Hyde continued.

"Nope," Tom replied, seemingly now more at ease. "Did hear something about that marshal."

"And Luke?" Zoe asked, turning to him.

"No, ma'm, just him. Come in town alone, fellow in a saloon was telling me. Reckon he left Luke waiting outside in the bushes."

"What'd he say about the marshal?"

Tom smiled, obviously enjoying his moments as the center of attention. "Seems he come into this here saloon for a drink. Was some soldiers there. One of them got to rawhiding the marshal about some friend of his. Ended up with the marshal pistol-whipping him something fierce. When he got done doing that, he ups and dares the rest of the soldiers to draw on him."

"They call his hand?" Crow wondered.

"Nope, sure didn't. Let him walk right out of the place —and I sort of got the idea everybody was plenty glad to see him go. . . . You seen any sign of him and Luke yet?"

"No," the girl answered with a sigh.

"We're getting close," Walt Crow said hurriedly. "Expect we've gained a-plenty. Sure ain't no time to be quitting now."

"Not planning to," Zoe said. "I think in another day or so we'll have them in sight."

"One thing for certain," Hyde said, rubbing at his jaw, "them vittles are going to come in handy. We ain't had a square meal since we left Boston City."

"That sure is the truth!" Crow added. "Some mighty fine camping places along the old Rio, too, so we can

start figuring on a good place to haul up and have ourselves a real supper, ain't that right, lady?"

Zoe nodded. They all needed a good meal, there was
no doubt of that. The horses, too, could stand a rest and
a treat of river grass with all the water they wanted.
They had made do with range feed and very little to
drink for several days.

But she did hate to lose the time. They should keep
moving as they had been, well up until near midnight
and then pulling out next morning around first light; the
steady pressing was beginning to tell on the horses—and
on her, she knew, but the need within her was a driving
force and difficult to restrain.

Curly and Walt Crow, however, didn't appear to be affected much and she reckoned they were more or less
accustomed to such hardship. The whiskey—their supply
seemed to be inexhaustible—possibly had something to
do with their endurance, but undoubtedly a big meal
would be of benefit to them.

Thus fortified, and with a night's rest behind the horses,
they should be able to make better time, even catch up
with Rye and Luke before they reached the Arizona border. Zoe smiled wryly. What then? How would she go
about finishing the task of freeing Luke?

She had a lot of gall thinking she could accomplish what
no other man had ever been able to do—take a prisoner
away from John Rye. What made her believe she could
effect such wonderwork? Was it because, being a woman,
she unconsciously felt that Rye would not accord her the
same ruthless treatment he reputedly employed when
dealing with a man?

She was not aware of any such feeling, Zoe assured herself—and she certainly wasn't going to depend on it. She'd manage an escape for Luke by using her wits, not any womanly wiles.

Zoe looked ahead. They were well within the canyon now, with steep, rocky slopes lifting up to high, craggy peaks and ledges around which thin clouds drifted. There was little vegetation growing on the rugged surfaces but a small stream flowed along the floor of the deep slash supplying moisture for cottonwoods, cedars and numberless shrubs growing along its banks.

"Reckon we could camp here," Crow suggested a bit hopefully. "Some real good spots."

The girl shook her head. "Several hours of daylight left —and I want to be on the other side of the river when we stop. How much farther is it?"

"The Rio? Ten, twelve mile."

"We'll keep going."

John Rye would not be calling a halt in the middle of the afternoon, she could be sure of that. He would start early, and ride late, and if she were to overtake him she must do no less. Too, if the only plan she had, which was to ambush him, was to be a practical one, they would not only have to catch up, but pass and get in front of him.

They rode on, climbing up out of the canyon and coming onto a long, grassy mesa that sloped gently down to the floor of a valley green with trees and through which a river sparkled. A row of extinct volcanoes stood like dark, frowning sentinels on its opposite side, and far, far to the west a snow-topped mountain lifted its peak against the steel-blue sky.

"Is that in Arizona?" Zoe asked.

Hyde, who had made several trips through the country, said, "Nope, that's what they call Taylor Mountain, and it's still in New Mexico. Arizona's still a lot a miles past it . . . Don't go that way, anyhow. We got to cut south, down the valley, following the river 'til we come to Socorro. Then we swing west."

"It's a long trip," she murmured. "Seems we've been riding forever."

"For a fact—"

They slanted across the broad mesa, keeping the wisps of smoke rising from the settlement well to their right, and forded the river near an Indian pueblo.

"Heard tell they're friendlies," Hyde said, "but we best stay clear of them. Never know for sure what a redskin'll take it in his head to do."

Shortly after sundown Zoe called a halt in a grassy clearing on the west bank of the stream. There was unlimited grazing and water for the worn horses and plenty of firewood for their own use. The valley was warm and the air was soft, and it would be the best and most comfortable camp they had set up.

Dismounting, she turned to the men. "We won't find a better place," she began, and then stopped, a frown clouding her face. "Where's Tom?"

Crow, off his saddle, leaned against the bay he was riding, made an offhand gesture. "Pulled out," he said with a half grin. "Figured he'd come far enough. Expect he wanted to see what Albuquerque looked like."

Zoe considered the two men coldly. There was something in their manner that disturbed, even frightened her a little.

"Said to say his good-bys to you and hoping you good luck," Hyde added. He was still mounted, was slumped forward, forearm resting on the saddle horn.

Zoe's eyes snapped. "I don't believe a word you're telling me! He wouldn't have gone off like that without coming to me himself. My guess is you ran him off."

Crow threw up his hands in mock astonishment. "Why, lady, why'd we do something like that?"

"You've got your reasons—I'm no dewy-eyed kid! When he showed up back there in the canyon, I thought you looked a bit surprised and put out—like you didn't expect him to find us."

Crow, palms still spread in bewilderment, turned to Curly Hyde. "Just can't figure what's making her say something like that, can you? . . . And us being so good to her, and all that."

"Sure can't. Man'd think she'd appreciate us more."

Zoe, lips set, reached into her pocket and, drawing her pistol, thrust it under the waistband of her baggy trousers. The uneasiness had passed. She had handled their kind before, many times; she could do it again.

"You're damned poor liars—both of you," she said evenly. "You got rid of Tom because you didn't want him around. Well, you best take a warning—it makes no difference. Make a wrong move toward me—either one of you—and you'll end up with a bullet in your belly."

11

Outlaws or lawmen? Rye gave that only fleeting thought as the rider to the left of center threw up his arms, went off his saddle backwards. The double charge of buckshot had caught him straight on. Immediately, the remaining men, who and whatever they were, spread out, and crouched low on their horses, laid down a steady hail of bullets.

Jamming the shotgun back into the boot, Rye drew his pistol, began to return their fire as he spurred to pull abreast of Braden. He could not hope to hold off the riders for long. They wanted Luke dead and were making it plain they intended to bring such about regardless of the cost.

Alongside the outlaw, Rye pointed to a dark band of trees some distance to their right. A house, with its collection of smaller structures, lay off its lower end, while on beyond them a row of red-faced bluffs lifted above the rolling contour of the land.

"Head for that grove!" the lawman shouted.

Braden, hunched low, manacled hands clutching the horn of his saddle, twisted about. His eyes were bright with fear and his features were strained.

"Then what?" he shouted, flinching as a bullet plucked at his sleeve.

"Try and lose them—that's what!" Rye yelled back. "Got a chance once we're off this flat."

He looked around. They had gained slightly on the riders. The squat redhead who appeared to be the leader of the bunch, had fallen back a few yards. Again Rye wondered who they were; if lawmen, it seemed they would have identified themselves and made the fact known; such was customary.

But Luke Braden was a killer, and a desperate one. For all they knew, he was traveling with another outlaw, no better than himself. They could have spotted Luke and, assuming that to be the fact, elected to move in, taking no chances. A grimness came over Rye. If that was true, he had just killed a fellow lawman. He felt a twinge of regret, passed it off; there was no reason to blame himself. The posse, if that's what they were, shouldn't have been in such a hurry to use their guns.

Steadying himself as best he could while the chestnut thundered over the grassy lifts and falls of the mesa in the wake of Braden's black, Rye triggered two quick shots at the nearest of the riders. The bullets fanned close. The man, a slim, wiry-looking individual, jerked aside, almost swerved into a companion.

Accuracy was next to an impossibility for all of them, luck actually being the prime factor. The fast pace of the horses, the rolling, brushy land made it more a matter of staying on the saddle than shooting. He'd better reload the shotgun, have it ready, Rye decided, and, holstering the pistol, pulled the double-barrel from its scabbard once again.

The trees loomed nearer. Breaking the shotgun, Rye

dug into his saddlebags, came up with a handful of shells. Slipping cartridges into the empty chambers, he tipped the weapon upward, rested it against his shoulder. He was hoping it would not be necessary to use it again—at least not until he knew who the redhead was and what he and the men with him wanted. Maybe, once they reached the shelter of the grove he could manage to talk to them, or to Luke.

Bullets continued to thunk into the soil, sending up small geysers of dust and trash, and clipping through the clumps of rabbit bush, snakeweed and other mesa growth. They'd been fortunate so far; neither of them had been touched and both horses had also escaped injury. Such good luck wouldn't hold indefinitely. The law of averages was bound to work against them and one of the bullets was sure to find its target.

One had. Even as John Rye shifted his attention to Braden with words of instruction on his lips, he saw the outlaw recoil. Suddenly angered, the marshal twisted about. Hastily leveling the shotgun, he fired directly at the oncoming riders. The range was not good—too far to be really effective—but he gave that no thought as he rushed to overtake Braden's slowing horse.

Luke turned an agonized face toward him. Blood was spreading across his shoulder, staining the back of his jacket.

"I'm hit—"

Rye nodded. "Keep going . . . Cut left soon's we're in the. trees!"

He roweled the chestnut again, pulled away from the outlaw. The grove was not as thick as he'd hoped but there were some large trees and the brush, while not tall, stood in dense thickets here and there. He looked back. Braden, almost flat on his saddle, hands locked to the horn, was sawing dangerously as the black whipped back and forth, avoiding the pines and the clumps of oak.

Beyond him the redhead and his men were just entering the grove, necessarily slowing as they left the open ground and began to encounter the growth. Rye veered hard right as if to gain the protection of the bluffs on the far side of the area. Braden's horse followed obediently.

A dozen yards and the lawman doubled back sharply, wheeled in behind a ragged mound of rocks and false sage and other brush. He jerked the chestnut to a stop and, as Luke's black crowded in, he reached out, seized the lead rope dangling from its bridle.

Immediately, he moved on, now cutting back towards the flat, keeping the horses at a slow, quiet walk. Luke stared at him anxiously.

"What are you doing? You're heading for—"

"Shut up!" Rye snapped in a low voice.

Over to their left he could hear the crashing of the riders hurrying through the grove. They had reached the opposite side of the hill, appeared to be continuing on in the direction of the bluffs. The marshal drew to a halt. Listening intently to the fading sounds, he broke the shotgun, threw aside the spent shells and reloaded.

"We're behind them," he said, satisfied. "We can lose them now."

Braden shook his head violently. "No! You got to go after them while you got a chance—use that scatter-gun, kill them—like you did Red Dog!"

Rye settled back slowly on his saddle, fixed his cold

eyes on Luke. "Who the hell are they?" he demanded in a voice taut with impatience.

Braden stirred weakly. "The whole bunch—they're out to get me."

"I can see that. Why? They lawmen or friends of yours?"

"Ain't neither one," the outlaw mumbled. "How about doing something to my arm? It's hurting like hell."

"I will—after I know who that bunch is."

The sounds of the riders passing had died into the distance. For a time they would not be troubled by them, but it would be wise to move on quickly; they would eventually discover their error and backtrack.

"Let's hear it," Rye said. "We're sitting right here until I know who I'm up against."

Luke mopped at his face with a forearm. "I reckon you could call them friends—leastways they was once. The redheaded one's Pete Stanley. Others are Amos Cook and Ben Polk and Ollie King. One you shot was Red Dog Smith."

John Rye breathed easier. It had been no posse of lawmen. "What kind of friends want you dead?"

Braden again swiped at the sweat glistening on his features. "They was with me on that bank holdup."

"One where you killed that woman and her two boys?"

The outlaw murmured an affirmative. He needed to go no further; understanding was coming quickly to the marshal. The gang, except for Luke, had escaped, killing two lawmen on the street during the process. Their identities were still unknown.

"They're scared you'll talk—that it?"

Braden nodded. "Made a fool mistake. When I got sentenced to hang I let it out that I'd spill my guts about who my partners were if it come to where they was putting a rope around my neck. Figured that way Pete and them would sure break me out so's I couldn't name them . . . Goddammit, Marshal, I'm bleeding to death. Ain't you—"

"You'll live . . . Instead of breaking you out, they're aiming to kill you to keep you quiet."

"Yeh. Second time they've tried. Best thing you can do is slip up on them from behind and blast the whole bunch with that scatter-gun."

"Not much of a hand at murder," Rye said dryly, sliding the weapon back into its boot.

"Hell—they're guilty as me—"

"Not saying they aren't, but it'll be handled another way."

The lawman paused, listened into the warm hush. Birds were flitting about in the trees but his attention centered on the area of the bluffs, where a pale cloud of dust was hanging in the sky. Stanley and the others were still searching in that part of the country.

Reaching down, he took up the black's lead rope, and, touching the chestnut with his rowels, began to move off through the grove. Braden protested at once.

"This here arm of mine—ain't you fixing—?"

"We'll head down to that house, get it doctored there," the marshal replied.

Ordinarily ranchers and homesteaders were friendly to lawmen, rendered aid when it was requested. Too, it would be a good place to hole up for a few hours if Pete Stanley and the others continued to search the grove.

12

Zoe turned back to her horse, and, taking down the sacks of grub and getting the coffeepot and cups, she returned to the center of the clearing. The scar-faced Crow and Curly Hyde were standing beside the latter's mount talking quietly. The situation would come to a head that night, she realized, and if she found herself unable to keep the pair in hand, she'd strike out on her own.

"Here, let me do that," Crow said, pulling away from his partner and crossing to where she was raking sticks and other dry litter together for a fire.

Zoe drew back, centered her attention on the food Tom Horn had brought. Taking out bacon, bread, potatoes, a tin of peaches and one of tomatoes, she placed all on a flat rock.

"The kid forget that there frying pan you was wanting?" Crow asked, pausing.

The girl shook her head, drew the utensil from the sack and placed it over the fire, now beginning to catch.

"You'll be needing a knife," Crow said, and handed her the sheathed blade hanging from his belt.

Walt was endeavoring to put her at ease with a fine show of co-operation and friendliness, Zoe thought as she sliced strips of the fat bacon into the spider for grease. The next thing he'd be offering to cook the meal; but he didn't. Instead, he got to his feet and wandered off toward the horses.

Zoe watched him rejoin Hyde, a little of the tenseness leaving her. The show of strength and her continual rebuffs perhaps had done some good. Maybe the pair would put their minds back to the rescuing of Luke now and forget about her being a woman.

With the bacon beginning to sizzle, filling the still air with its good aroma, she hurriedly peeled several potatoes, thin sliced them into the pan. The flames were too close, and looking about she found a number of small rocks which she added to the firebox Crow had arranged and thus raised the spider to where the food would cook slower.

That done, she then filled the coffeepot with water, placed it where it could heat, turned next to cutting off thick slices of bread to be fried in the skillet later.

She could see nothing of Curly and Walt, both having led their horses to the river for a watering. They had not offered to take care of her buckskin, but she guessed one of them would do so later. . . . She'd relieve them of the responsibility, Zoe decided; the fewer favors done for her by them, the better. Leaving the food, she dropped back to her mount.

Starting to remove the saddle, Zoe hesitated, having second thought as to the wisdom of such. With matters between her and the two men at a precarious point, she might want to depart on short notice. It would be well to leave the gear in place. The buckskin could get by for one night.

Tucking the end of the cinch strap back into place, she

led the animal down to the river, and while he was sat-
isfying his needs, she quickly filled her canteen. Minutes
later, when she returned to the camp, the men were
hunched beside the fire. Hyde, as usual, clutched a bottle
of whiskey in one of his big hands, watched her approach
through hooded, speculative eyes, while Crow, stirring
the meat and potatoes about in the spider with his knife,
looked up and shook his head.

"Was aiming to do that for you."

"It's done," she replied shortly, and, waiting until he
had pulled back out of the way, set to work making the
coffee.

The potatoes and bacon combination looked dry. Picking up the canteen Crow had put nearby for her use, Zoe
added a small amount of water to the skillet, opened the
cans of tomatoes and peaches and set out the coffee cups,
both men watching her closely, following her every move.

"We don't have plates," she said, fully aware of their
attention. "No forks either. Use the cups and your
fingers."

"Fingers was made before forks," Hyde prattled, putting his bottle down and, taking one of the tin containers,
filled it from the skillet. "How about a chunk of that
bread?"

In the interests of getting the meal over quickly, Zoe
decided she'd forgo the usual custom of frying the bread
to soften it, and laying out several slices where they
would be handy to the men, she portioned out a quantity
of the food for herself.

Throughout it all she kept a wary eye on the pair,
staying beyond arm's reach of either, not knowing what

she could expect and accordingly taking no chances. Crow and Hyde seemed to have interest only in the food she'd prepared, however, and the supper passed with hardly any conversation and no suspicious moves on their part.

After it was all over, and with the butt of her pistol showing plainly above the waistband of her trousers, Zoe found a place back from the fire—scarcely needed for warmth since the night was balmy—to enjoy a final cup of coffee. The two men sprawled out on the opposite side of the low flames, the bottle between them.

"Ought to be catching up with Luke and that marshal, come sundown tomorrow," Hyde said. "Sure can't be much behind them now."

It was good to hear that. She was anxious to find Rye, make an effort to free her husband, and, failing or not, have done with it. The hardships and inconveniences of the trail, of constantly being in the saddle and on the move, the ever present threat of problems with the two men accompanying her, were steadily wearing her down. The sooner she could get it all over with, make her way to some town where she could pick up where she'd left off living the way a woman should, the better.

"What're you and Luke aiming to do when we get that marshal off'n his back and out of the way?"

"Luke can do what he pleases," the girl replied indifferently, without thinking. "We're finished."

Walt Crow sat up. His lips cracked into a broad grin. "Do tell! He know that?"

"No," she answered, biting her lips. It was a foolish thing to have said, amounting to nothing less than opening the door to them insofar as Luke was concerned. If the fact that she was the wife of a friend had placed any restraint upon them at all, it was gone now.

"We're right sorry to hear that," Hyde said, "but we're mightly glad, too. Means you're sort of on your own."

"Forget it," Zoe snapped. "Nothing's changed far as you, or any other man's concerned. I'm a card dealer, not a saloon girl looking for business."

"Hell, we know that," Crow said, a thread of sarcasm in his tone. "Why, any fool can just look at you and see you're pure quality—a genuine lady."

Curly laughed. "Ain't no doubt of that! You want a drink of my liquor, lady?"

Ignoring the offer, Zoe studied the pair narrowly. It wouldn't be long—she could see the trouble coming. A few more pulls at the bottle and she'd have them both to contend with—and it would be sheer stupidity to wait until that point was reached.

Tossing the last of the coffee into the brush, the girl rose to her feet. Walt Crow's head came up instantly.

"You turning in?"

"Not yet," she said, fighting to keep her voice even. "Going to walk down to the river and back, first. That all right with you?"

Both men laughed. Crow wagged his head. "Ain't she the one!"

"The beatenest!" Curly agreed. "Now, don't you let none of them Indians grab you, honey! They do, you just sing out and me'n Walt'll come running!"

She would have to leave the sack of grub, the coffee-pot, her cup—everything—Zoe realized as she moved leisurely back into the brush. To collect them, carry them to the buckskin, standing a few yards off in the darkness, would arouse their suspicions. But that was a small price to pay for escape; she'd manage—she always had and she'd do so now.

Reaching the horse Zoe quietly untied the halter rope, and, wheeling, carefully led the animal toward the river. She was well below the two men, and while they could not see her because of the brush and trees, they would be able to hear. She could only hope that any sounds the buckskin made would be attributed to her.

The flat shine of the stream appeared before her. Immediately she went to the saddle. She'd head down the river for a mile or so, then cut back to the trail. The thud of the buckskin's hooves might still be audible to them through the hush even then, but she'd have a good lead and with a little luck she should be able to make good her escape.

Abruptly she checked the buckskin. Back along the stream she caught the vague outlines of the horses Hyde and Crow were riding. If they had no mounts, there would be no pursuit—and she could forget about them being on her trail.

Coming off the saddle, Zoe ground-reined her horse, and, again with extreme care, worked through the heavy growth to the dozing animals. Reaching them, she threw a glance toward the camp. Hyde lay stretched out in the fire's glare while Walt Crow was sloshing the remainder of the coffee about in the pot, apparently considering the need to add more water and set it back on the flames to boil.

Taking the picket ropes in her hand, Zoe pivoted, and, choosing her path carefully, she led the two horses to where the buckskin waited. Tension gripping her, pulling each nerve to wire tautness, she climbed once more onto the saddle, and with the two weary animals plodding along behind, struck off along the path that followed the bank of the Rio.

With each passing moment her spirits lifted, but she resolutely denied the urge to quicken the pace. Best to take it slow until she'd placed a safe distance between herself and the camp and then—

"Hey!" It was Walt Crow's voice. "She's running off—and she's stealing the horses!"

13

As they rode into the homesteader's yard a thin, graying, work-scarred woman appeared in the doorway of the crude sod and timber house. She stared at them suspiciously.

"Got a man here that's been shot," Rye called. "We can use a little help."

The woman looked over her shoulder into the dark interior of the low-roofed structure. Presently a man stepped to her side. He was tall, somewhat stooped, and like her showed the signs of never ending labor.

"Who are you?" he demanded in a rough voice.

"Name's Rye. I'm a U. S. Marshal. Man here's my prisoner."

The homesteader gave that thought, finally nodded. "I reckon it's all right," he said. "Bring him on in."

The lawman got off the chestnut, and, taking a moment to obtain the leg irons from his saddlebags, released Luke Braden's manacles. The outlaw groaned as he dismounted, and, leaning heavily against the marshal, allowed himself to be taken into the house.

The woman had pulled back one of the two chairs placed at a slab table built into the wall and was standing by, hands on hips, watching narrowly.

"I'm Virgil Patterman," the homesteader said, and,

jerking a thumb at the woman, added, "This here's my wife. Name's Emma. How'd your prisoner get shot? You do it?"

"Some of his friends," Rye answered, taking a loop around the table's thick center leg with the chain and snapping the ankle cuffs in place. For the time being he'd let the manacles hang loose. "Be needing some hot water and cloth for a bandage."

Patterman bucked his head at his wife, who obediently crossed to the four-hole cookstove in a back corner of the room. Taking a pan she filled it with steaming water from a kettle and brought it to the table. Setting it in front of Braden, she went then to a stack of shelves on the wall that served as a chest of drawers, procured a strip of white cotton cloth.

"I'll tend him," she said gruffly, brushing Rye aside. "Ain't never seen a man who could do something like this right yet."

The lawman stepped back and watched her remove Luke's jacket and shirt. The injury didn't appear to be serious, the bullet having passed through the fleshy part of his upper arm. It had bled copiously but other than that there was no problem.

Reaching down for the wrist cuff dangling from the outlaw's unhurt arm, Rye snapped it about the slack in the leg chain. Virgil Patterman frowned.

"What're you doing that for? Already got him chained up like he was a dog."

"That's the way I want him," Rye said coolly, and, moving to the door, stepped out into the yard.

For a long minute he listened for any indication that

Pete Stanley and the rest of Braden's one-time friends had given up on the bluffs and were back in the grove. He could neither hear nor see any evidence of such, but there was no doubt in his mind that the outlaws were still in the neighborhood, carefully searching.

Accordingly, Rye crossed to the horses and, leading both, took them to the yard behind the Patterman house and picketed them inside one of the larger sheds that apparently served as a barn in times past. Out of sight, the chestnut and the black would go unnoticed should Stanley pay casual attention to the homestead. If the outlaws rode in to investigate before Luke was ready to travel, it would be a different matter.

Such could very well prove to be the case, the lawman decided, and, pulling the shotgun from its boot, he hung it under an arm and retraced his steps to the house.

Emma Patterman had washed and cleaned Braden's wound, applied some sort of dark antiseptic and was in the process of binding it with strips of cloth when the marshal entered.

He flicked Luke with a critical glance. "You about ready to ride?"

The woman squared around, faced him defiantly. "He ain't going nowheres, mister. He starts riding, that there hole's going to start bleeding again."

"Let it," Rye said bluntly. "Those friends of his are still out there somewhere—and they'll be coming here for a look. I want to be gone by then, for your sake as well as mine."

"If they're friends, why'd they shoot him?" Patterman asked, cocking his head slyly to one side.

"One good reason—they want him dead."

The homesteader drew himself up to his full height, crossed his arms. "That ain't how he tells it."

Rye glanced at Braden. There was a smirk on the outlaw's bearded face. "I'm not interested in what he says."

"Well, we are," Patterman declared. "Claims you're taking him back to the pen, where they're going to hang him for something he ain't done. Them friends of his are trying to help him get away from you. Says his wife's in on it, too, that she's got a couple more friends who're out to stop you."

The lawman studied Luke Braden thoughtfully, his sardonic features dark, almost satanic. "You've been right busy talking—"

The outlaw stirred. "True—everything I told them."

"About your wife, maybe, but not about Pete Stanley and the others—or your being innocent."

"Says you're getting a big reward for taking him in. That's why you're keeping him chained up close—like he was an animal."

"He's worse—"

"He's a man, and it ain't human," Patterman broke in angrily. "Just 'cause you're a lawman don't give you no right to treat him like you're doing!"

Rye stepped back to the doorway, listened into the warm day. The only sound was the far-off whistling of a meadowlark. Pivoting, he started toward Braden, halted. Virgil Patterman was leveling a rifle at him.

"I'll thank you for that scatter-gun," the homesteader said quietly. "Pistol, too."

Rye smiled bleakly. "I don't think so, friend. If you want to die, try taking them."

"I won't be the only one dying—"

"Maybe not. Meantime you'd best think about what it'll mean to throw down on a lawman. Can get you a few years behind bars—if you live."

Patterman shifted uneasily, glancing at Braden, then at his wife standing beside the outlaw. Luke's eyes were filled with cunning and a tautness stretched the skin of his face.

"He can't do nothing to you specially if he's dead," the outlaw pointed out in a husky voice. "If you're scared of pulling that trigger, give me that gun. I'll do it."

The homesteader frowned. "Can't do that," he said hesitantly. "Wouldn't be right—no more than him treating you like he is."

The break in Patterman's manner was not lost to Rye. "Put the rifle down," he said gently. "I don't want any trouble with you any more than you want some with the law. If you're interested, I've got papers telling who this man is and why I'm taking him back to Yuma Prison to hang. He's a killer—the worst kind, if there is such a thing."

"What'd he do?"

"Him and his friends held up a bank. He shot down a widow woman and her two little boys who happened to be there at the time. His friends killed two deputy sheriffs. They got away but he was caught. He was tried in court and sentenced to hang."

"It wasn't a fair trial," Braden muttered. "Every one of them on the jury was against me because I was an outsider. And that there judge—he's one of them that hangs every man they bring up before him."

"It doesn't end there," Rye went on. "A lawman was taking him to Yuma. Stopped at a homesteader's—place just like yours—to water their horses. He got to talking to the fellow, hornswoggled him into believing he was being treated bad, same as he's done you. Man tried to help him. In the scuffling Braden there grabbed up a sickle. Killed the lawman, then done the same to the homesteader and got away."

Rye finished, his cold gaze never leaving the face of Patterman. The homesteader swallowed hard.

"That all set down on them papers you said you had?"

"Every bit of it."

The tall man turned to Braden. "Is it the God's truth?"

The outlaw shrugged. "Aw, go to hell," he said in an exhausted voice.

From somewhere back along the edge of the grove a gunshot echoed. The lawman drew up quickly. It would be Stanley summoning the others, making ready to search elsewhere. Immediately he stepped up to Luke, and, producing the necessary keys, unlocked the leg chain and the handcuff attached to it.

"On your feet!"

Patterman, rifle lowered, drew back. Emma, unmoving, held her ground beside the outlaw as if unwilling to permit his departure. Rye shouldered her out of the way, the need to be out of the house, mounted and riding before the outlaws could put in an appearance, pushing at him urgently.

"Obliged to you for your trouble," he said, shoving Luke toward the door.

Patterman nodded dumbly. "Sure, sure," he mumbled as Rye propelled Braden into the open.

The outlaw abruptly braced himself and came to a stumbling halt. Whirling, he faced the homesteader.

"I ain't forgetting this!" he shouted.

"Keep going," Rye snarled, pointing at the horses. "What you'd best do is remember there's four of your kind out there coming to kill you. Against those odds, I'd be smart to just go on and let them have you."

14

Gunshots racketed through the night. Zoe smiled tightly. Crow and Curly Hyde were simply emptying their pistols in her direction, venting their anger and frustration.

She rode on, hurrying as much as possible, but the horses she was leading continually and stubbornly held back. Finally, at a safe distance, she released their ropes, and, swinging in behind them, drove them ahead of her. This worked well for almost a mile and then one of the animals swerved off the path, trotting off toward a line of hills looming up on her right.

The second horse followed shortly. Zoe slowed the buckskin, gave it a few moments' thought and came to the conclusion that going after them wasn't worth the effort and time that would be lost. She was a good two miles below the camp where she'd left Crow and Hyde stranded, and there was no possibility of them recovering their mounts until after daylight. Best she ride on, put as much distance between herself and them as possible.

It was a relief to be rid of the two men. Like as not both would have backed down when they came to grips with John Rye, for she was now fully convinced their interest in freeing Luke was secondary to other motives they had in mind, if, indeed, it ever existed at all. And as far as her needing them as guides, that no longer was necessary; she had the route the lawman would be following firmly fixed in her memory just from listening to Curly.

She must continue southward, keeping along the river until near Socorro. There she should turn west, striking a line for Silver City. It was the only trail Rye could possibly take, Hyde had said, but it would be necessary to overtake him and his prisoner before they crossed into Arizona since it would be difficult, short of tracking, to determine the route he would choose to reach Yuma. Renegade Apaches were pretty much on the loose, Curly had warned, and a man would have to pick his own way, ignoring the established trails along which the marauding redskins were known to lie in wait for unsuspecting pilgrims, if he expected to stay alive.

Zoe rode on steadily through the half dark. Once she heard riders in the night but they were moving in the opposite direction and were farther west. Evidently the main road lay there; she resisted the impulse to swing onto it in the interests of easier, faster traveling, deciding it would be better if no one saw her. In that way no word could reach her erstwhile companions should they make inquiries.

Near dawn she halted at the edge of a small backwater pond to rest the buckskin and ease her own aching muscles. She was not hungry, thus the lack of food was no problem, but she would have enjoyed a cup of hot, black coffee.

She remained there for an hour or so and then with a smoke streamer twisting up from a settlement on to the south, which she took to be Socorro, she began to angle

westward. Eventually such a course would intersect with
the Silver City trail, she reasoned, and she would once
again be closing in on John Rye.

The day wore on, became increasingly warmer as the
sun cut its path through a sky filled with scattered, thin
clouds. She met no one, saw no one in the shimmering
distances, and by midafternoon found herself having dif-
ficulties in staying on the slowly plodding buckskin.

She called a halt beside a bushy cedar, refreshed herself by soaking her brightly colored scarf in water from
the canteen and bathing her face and neck. The buckskin nuzzled her anxiously while she was doing so and
she satisfied his need to some extent by swabbing his
lips and nostrils with the wet cloth and forcing a small
amount of the water into his mouth in the way she'd
seen her father do.

She was careful to waste none of it; Hyde had made
no mention of another river along the trail, but surely
water would be available once she reached the mountains
stretching high and dark green far ahead; she needed
only to conserve what was left in the canteen until then.

The sun dropped lower but the mountains seemed to
draw no closer. The land had changed somewhat, however; the stark mesa had fallen behind her and she had
gradually entered into a more fertile country, one with
dense groves of trees, deep, grassy swales and low,
round-topped hills. Farther south it appeared to be even
more inviting but the girl ignored an inclination to alter,
to turn toward that attraction; Silver City and Arizona
lay due west and she would not, under any circumstances,
vary from her chosen course.

Her thoughts turned to Walt Crow and Curly Hyde. She wondered if they had found their horses by that hour. It was likely. Curly was a good tracker. She only hoped the animals had continued to wander on through the hills and had not doubled back to the river, thus making it more difficult for the men to find them.

Would they set out to overtake her? Zoe puzzled over that as she pressed on with the sun now a round, orange glare directly in her eyes. They could give it up, forget all about her and Luke, and turn back. They had nothing to gain other than personal satisfaction and she doubted that counted much with either of them. They were more likely to ride to one of the settlements close by, where liquor and willing saloon girls would be plentiful.

She drew up suddenly. Off to the left in a small valley stood a house. A homesteader, she guessed, judging from the small structures and the general appearance of the place. A sigh of relief passed through her; here, at last, was a bit of civilization where she could halt, rest, get food and reassure herself of her directions.

Urging the buckskin on, she descended the long, gentle slope and swung into the yard fronting the low-roofed house. Everything about the homestead looked worn, weathered, even the tall, stooped man and the slatternly woman who stepped into the doorway to view her approach skeptically.

Zoe nodded, smiled. "I'm going to Silver City—and I've lost my sack of groceries—grub. Could I get something to eat from you? I'll pay—"

"Get down," the man said at once. "I'll take care of your horse."

The girl dismounted quickly, crossed to the entrance of the hut. The man, without looking at her, gathered in the buckskin's reins.

"It'll cost a dollar—" he said.

"That will be all right," she replied, and entered the house.

The old woman, hands on hips, gray hair stringing down about her emaciated face, met her with set, curling lips.

"Ain't got nothing but rabbit stew and cornbread."

Zoe shrugged. "Fine. Some coffee would taste good."

The woman turned to the stove, and, using a tin cup as a ladle, dipped out a portion of a thin concoction into a cracked bowl and set it on a table built into the wall. Motioning for Zoe to take one of the chairs, she supplied a spoon and a large square of cornbread, wiped out the cup with a rag hanging near the stove and filled it with coffee—chicory, the girl soon discovered—from a battered enamel pot.

But she was grateful and, voicing no complaints, began to eat hungrily, enjoying every bite and swallow of the simple fare. The old woman settled onto the only other chair, studying her closely with her watery eyes. . . . A chicken wandered into the doorway, paused there, craning its neck as it searched the dirt floor for crumbs. The woman made a motion with the rag she still held in her bony hand, sent the bird back into the yard with a wild fluttering of its wings.

"You're a far piece from Silver City," she said then. "Ain't decent for no woman to be traveling alone. Ain't safe neither."

"You're the first people I've seen. Hardly think there's—"

"Well, been a-plenty coming by the last couple of days. Was a lawman and a prisoner he had all chained up. Then was four others—"

Zoe had come to attention. "That lawman—was his name Rye? Did he call his prisoner Luke?"

"Ain't sure. You'll have to ask the mister, was him done the talking to him. Why?"

"I'm trying to catch up with them."

The old woman's head came forward expectantly. "You got something to do with that prisoner he's taking to Yuma Prison for hanging—like maybe you're the wife he was telling about?"

It could only be Luke and the marshal, Zoe realized, but she weighed her reply carefully, not certain of what the woman's reaction would be. Before she could speak the man thumped up to the door and stepped inside.

"This here's that prisoner fellow's wife," the woman announced in a high, told-you-so sort of tone. "He was telling us the truth!"

The stooped homesteader considered Zoe silently. Then, crossing to the stove, he poured himself a cup of the chicory, leaned back against the wall.

"You his wife?" he asked.

Zoe nodded. "When were they here?"

"Yesterday, it was. That marshal telling us for true about what your man done?"

"I don't know what he said but I suppose it was."

"And you're aiming to set him free?"

"Expect to try . . . Was Luke—my husband—all right?"

"Been shot. Some friends of his'n tried to take him away from the marshal and put a bullet in his arm. My wife fixed it up. Weren't nothing bad."

"Friends?" the girl echoed, wonderingly.

"Was what the marshal called them. Had something to do with him being along when they robbed a bank."

"I don't think he done all them things that marshal said," the homesteader's wife declared stubbornly. "That lawman is just after a big reward. True, else his wife wouldn't be trying to help him."

Zoe, her hunger abruptly appeased, pushed back from the table, reached into her pocket for money to pay for the meal.

"Reckon I'm going to have to make that two dollars," the homesteader said. "Wasn't figuring on feed for the horse."

The girl added another coin to the one she'd selected, laid both beside the cracked bowl, and got to her feet.

"The marshal and my husband—did they head on west for Silver City?"

"Silver ain't exactly west of here," the man said, stepping up to collect the money. "More to the south, but I reckon the trail sort of runs that way for a spell."

"They take it?"

"Far as I know. Lit out in that direction. You going on tonight?"

Zoe nodded. "Where do I get on the trail?"

"About a half mile below here . . . Horse is in the barn. You want me to get him?"

"Never mind," the girl said. "I'll find him. Obliged to you for the supper."

"I'm obliged to *you*." The homesteader grinned, clinking the two silver dollars in his hand.

15

Luke Braden, hunched low, broke into a run for the shed.
Rye threw a long, searching glance toward the grove and
fell in behind him. Stanley and the three other outlaws
had halted at the edge of the trees and were having a discussion of some sort—probably one concerning where
next to search for their one-time partner and his captor.

Eventually they would swing by the Pattermans', there
was little doubt of that, but odds were this would be
reserved to the last since the small, barren place offered
little to anyone seeking a hiding place. He could have
remained there, Rye supposed, and chanced a shoot-out
with Stanley, but he would have been saddled with the
homesteader and his wife, as well as Luke Braden, so the
disadvantage would be his. Too, his job was to get
the man safely to Yuma Prison and any diversion from
that course was contrary to his single-mindedness of
purpose.

They reached the horses, led them into the open. Luke
went onto the saddle with no help, all at once most anxious to quit the area. Rye, cool and deliberate as always,
paused beside the outlaw and locked his hands to the
horn in usual fashion. Braden cursed wildly.

"You could forget that for now!" he shouted.

The lawman merely shrugged, and, turning, stepped

up onto the chestnut. He could not see the outlaw party from that point in the yard, his view being blocked by a brushy windbreak planted by Patterman, and, moving out a short distance beyond it, he again put his attention on the grove. Stanley and his three friends had settled their problem, loping down the long grade toward the homestead.

Rye's jaw tightened. They had apparently decided to have their look at the Patterman place first instead of searching further among the trees and the brushy hills to the north, as he'd thought.

It was a bit of bad luck he could have done without; given an hour's start he might have gained the mountains on to the west with his prisoner, well ahead of any pursuit, and then easily shaken the outlaws. Now he would be fortunate to get a couple of hundred yards beyond the homesteader's before being seen. But the cards had been dealt and there was nothing to be done but play out the hand. Wheeling, he spurred back to Braden.

"Let's go," he said, taking up the black's lead rope and flipping it to the man. "Got to run for it. I want you in front of me—"

"Which way?" Luke asked nervously.

Rye pointed to a dark band of pines at the base of the nearest mountain, a long mile or so in the distance.

"Those trees—move out!"

Braden raked the black sharply with his spurs. The gelding plunged forward. Rye swerved in close, and only a yard apart they pounded across the hard-pack lying back of the Patterman house and reached open country.

The lawman glanced over his shoulder as the horses

leveled off into a fast gallop. The homesteader's sheds and house were between them and the outlaws, blocking off all sign of their departure, but the benefit derived would be one of short duration. Once Stanley reached the yard he would be afforded a sweeping panorama of the flat as it stretched out to meet the mountains. He came back around at Luke's worried shout.

"They're going to see us—"

"Keep riding," the marshal replied.

They reached the trees—tall pines, a few scrub oaks, a scattering of piñon and cedar—drove straight into the shadow-filled wood with both horses blowing hard and flecked with sweat. Rye turned half about on the saddle. They were well within the forest, and Pete Stanley and his men, little more than halfway across the flat, could no longer observe their movements.

"Cut to the left—"

Obediently Luke Braden veered the black toward the south. The slope was before them now, rising gradually to meet a hogback of barren, gray rock high above. The outlaw pointed.

"Horses ain't going to make that! Mine's about done now."

"Not where we're going," Rye answered. "Swing around the bottom of it. There's a valley there."

He was having his own doubts concerning the horses, beginning to wonder if they could last for even that short distance. He could feel the chestnut trembling beneath him, and stumbling frequently. He brushed at the moisture misting his eyes . . . Best to take no chances on either horse falling, breaking a leg. He glanced about. A thick stand of oak and mountain mahogany crowded against a mass of rock lay a short distance off the trail.

"Braden—over here!" he shouted, and swung toward the ragged formation.

Luke, frowning, wheeled the black off the path and down into the slight swale. "Thought you said we'd—"

"Changed my mind—"

A gunshot flatted through the hush. Rye swore grimly. They had been spotted. Stanley, or one of the outlaws with him, by sheer chance, had caught a glimpse of them climbing for the hogback.

"Into the brush—fast!" the marshal snapped, cutting in behind his prisoner.

"Hell—they've seen us. Ain't no use—"

"All somebody got was a quick look. If we're lucky they'll think we kept going towards the hogback."

Braden spurred his exhausted horse into the heart of the brush, settled back on the saddle. His face was shining with sweat and there was fear in his eyes.

"Like being in a trap, stopping here. Pete and them'll find us for sure."

"Not if you keep your mouth shut and that horse quiet," Rye said, dismounting. Drawing his shotgun from the boot, he moved to the edge of the rocks.

Braden stirred anxiously. "Unlock these here cuffs and give me a gun, and we can take care of the whole bunch when they go riding by."

"Not about to," the lawman said. "All I'm interested in is getting them off my back."

"Hell, they was in on that bank holdup, same as me."

"But you're the one I was sent after, and I aim to do

the job. If the law wants me to run them down, it'll be another time. . . . Button your lip. Sound carries plenty far up here. They might hear you talking."

Grumbling, Braden lapsed into silence. John Rye, shotgun cradled in his arms, hunched behind the brush-studded rocks. Through the tangled growth he could see the trail up which they had come no more than fifty feet in the distance. The outlaws would be passing along it, and, as Luke had said, he would have a clean sweep with his weapons. Adding four more prisoners to his string would be foolhardy, however; getting Braden to Yuma Prison came first.

The dull, solid thud of hooves reached him. He cast a warning glance at Braden, saw that the man had also heard. He need have no fear that Luke would betray their presence; to do so meant sudden death for himself. It was the horses moving unexpectedly that presented a danger, and if such occurred and the outlaws' attention was drawn to them, he'd have no choice but to open up on them.

"Keep going!"

The voice was harsh, impatient. Likely the speaker was Pete Stanley, dissatisfied with the slowness of the climb and fearful the man he needed to see dead for the sake of his own life, would again escape.

A horse came into view, head low and bobbing wearily as he fought the steep grade. Immediately behind him a second appeared, its rider, a rifle ready in his hands, throwing glances from side to side . . . Pete Stanley . . . It was the first good look he'd had at the redhead. He would know him well thereafter.

The two remaining riders, one a husky, dark and elderly man, the other much younger, were a few paces back, and as the line strung out along the path, Stanley twisted around, glared angrily at the pair.

"Get up here closer! You're dragging like a bunch of old women."

The older of the pair shrugged. "What the hell difference it make? We're coming, ain't we?"

"It'll make a hell of a lot of difference when we spot them two!" Stanley snarled. "I want you cracking down on them with everything you've got—everybody. I'm not planning to let them get away again!"

"You see!" Braden said in a hoarse whisper as the outlaws moved on by. "They're aiming to blast both of us, not just me! You're a damned fool not to cut them down while you got a chance!"

Rye said nothing. He simply watched the riders continue on up the trail. When they were finally lost to both sight and sound, he returned to the chestnut and mounted. Luke stared at him in disbelief.

"You figuring to leave here?"

"Sure," the lawman replied, reaching for the black's lead rope. "They're gone."

With the outlaw in tow he rode out of the brush and regained the trail. There he swung right, struck a course back down the narrow path over which they had just come.

"Thought we was heading for Silver City," Braden said at once.

Rye shrugged. "That's what Stanley's thinking."

Luke's relief was apparent. The men who sought to

kill him were heading off into one direction, they were taking the opposite. He grinned.

"Old Pete's sure going to cuss when he finds out he's been tricked. . . . But what about grub? You was aiming to stock up in Silver."

"Other towns around," the lawman replied. "Be coming to one before dark. Expect I'll get what we need there."

"Any chance we can go in together, get us a square meal and sleep in a real bed—?"

"Nope; same as Cimarron. I'll find a place for you to wait."

Luke groaned. "Means getting chained to a stump or something—"

The marshal nodded. "Gagged, too, if there's a need. But I don't think you're that dumb. Pete and the others may just get wise that they're on the wrong track and double back. If they heard you yelling it'd—"

"Won't be no need for a gag," Braden cut in. "Just you don't be gone too long."

16

Hyde had said the trail Rye and Luke would be taking ran due west; that was good enough for Zoe Braden and when she reached a fork at the foot of the first wall of mountains, one barely noticeable in the fading light, she kept to the right, continued on into the darkly silhouetted peaks and shadowy slopes.

The buckskin began to lag in no time at all and she began a program of alternately halting for a half hour or so to let the animal rest, and then moving on for a similar period of time. The system worked fairly well, enabling her to proceed through the night. For herself, she barely noticed fatigue, her body at that stage of weariness where numbness had taken over, or perhaps it was the belief she would soon overtake the lawman and her husband, and one way or another, it would all end.

Daylight found her well beyond the initial range of high, pine-clad hills and rocky ridges, and entering a wide, hilly valley rich with grass and periodically garnished with small groves and vivid patches of yellow and purple wild flowers. Around midmorning she saw smoke in the distance and concluded instantly that at last Silver City was in the offing.

Curly had been right insofar as the location of the town and the trail leading to it were concerned; she had

simply kept bearing straight into the direction in which
the sun had set, ignoring the homesteader's comment
that the settlement lay more to the south. She'd made
better time, too, than expected. That idea of hers of resting and riding for like periods had been a good one.

Thinking of Hyde swung her mind to him and his
partner, Walt Crow, and set her to wondering again what
had happened to them as the buckskin walked stolidly
on toward the spiral of smoke, gradually becoming more
definite. She'd seen the last of them, she hoped. Soon
after leaving Boston City, when she'd come to realize
what the intentions of the two men were, she had regretted enlisting their aid, and blamed herself for a lapse
in judgment. She was not so sure it was a mistake now;
it was because of them she had gotten this far, and done
so in record time.

The morning wore on, with the stops to rest the buckskin becoming more frequent and of longer duration. The
warmth of the sun and her own weariness and lack of
sleep were combining to finally overcome her now and
on several occasions she found herself dozing and awoke
with a start to discover the horse had stopped.

But she kept doggedly at it, moving through a world
of low brush-covered hills and arroyos, and flats covered
with a thin range grass upon which she saw small herds
of cattle grazing. The smoke had thickened and she
reckoned she was very near the settlement.

A rider appeared. Zoe pulled to a halt, something about
the man and horse striking a familiar chord in her mind.
A big man, shoulders squared in the driving sunlight;
flat-crowned hat rather than the high-peaked affairs so

common to the area; a powerful-looking horse, red-
brown—a chestnut she thought men termed the color.
God in heaven—it was John Rye!

A hand seemed to reach up from nowhere, grip her
by the throat as recognition came. For a long, breathless
span of moments she remained frozen, unable to think,
to act, and then abruptly she recovered, and, raking the
exhausted buckskin with her spurs, wheeled in behind
a mound upon which a family of bayonet yucca grew.

He had apparently been to the settlement, and since
he was alone it was only logical to assume he had left
Luke somewhere back along the way, safely trussed
and chained. A faint smile curved Zoe's lips as she dabbed
at the sweat on her cheeks with her scarf. She had only
to follow him at a reasonable distance and he'd lead her
to Luke.

Patient, she remained hidden by the yuccas until he
passed, some hundred yards or so below her. He was
riding up a shallow draw, pointing for a row of rock-
capped bluffs in front of which brush grew densely. When
he had moved out of sight, she swung the buckskin toward the draw, keeping well to the side and approaching at a long tangent.

Coming to the wash, she halted, dismounted and
quietly made her way forward on foot. There was no
sign of the lawman, but at the upper end of the sandy
gash she could see a small cabin built against the foot
of the reddish bluffs.

Zoe nodded in satisfaction. That was where Rye had
left Luke. Hurrying back to the buckskin, she once again
mounted, and, following out the angle of approach she'd

begun, cut through the choppy hills and came to the sagging old structure from the side.

Two horses stood at the end of the cabin, both tied to a small oak. There were no windows in that wall, and slipping quietly from the saddle, she led the buckskin up to them and tethered him to the same tree. Drawing her pistol, she then began a careful advance toward the door.

Midway she paused, looked down at the weapon in her hand, frowned. She was about to kill a man. Could she do it? Never before in her life had she used a weapon on a human being, and while accustomed to hearing of the deaths of men, even witnessing the shooting of two or three, she had never been a part of a killing. Could she kill John Rye now, even to accomplish her purpose—actually to win her own freedom?

A wave of determination came over her. She would have to, if it became necessary. Perhaps it would not; Rye was inside, likely involved in releasing Luke preparatory to resuming their journey. He would have no idea that she was around, or that he had been seen. It could be just a matter of holding the gun on him and ordering him to disarm himself and free Luke. She wasn't too clear what she'd do after that. Luke, if all the things she'd learned about him in the past few weeks were true, would undoubtedly want to kill Rye, thereby making certain the lawman could never again get on his trail.

She'd not permit that, she thought, moving on. She'd insist he'd not again commit murder, that he do no more than tie up the marshal—and not too securely, so that he would be able to free himself in time. They could take his horse, as she'd done those of Curly and Walt, thus leaving him afoot, and then ride on—but only to the next town.

There she'd make it clear to Luke that she was through, that she wanted no more to do with him and that he was to stay out of her life from that moment on under penalty of her calling in the law. Her obligation to him as a wife had been discharged, and that was the end of it.

A step away from the door Zoe halted. Her pulses were pounding and the butt of the pistol in her hand felt hot, sweaty, but she took a firmer grip on it. She'd come this far, she'd not back down now. Taking a deep breath, she reached for the limp rawhide string that would lift the latch.

"Drop the gun—"

Rye's cold voice and the unmistakable click of a weapon being cocked were like a blow to the back of her head. Rigid, she opened her fingers, allowed the pistol to fall. Immediately she heard the soft thud of his boot heels as he moved up beside her. A hand came against her shoulder, pushed her roughly aside, and then, bending down, he recovered the weapon and tucked it inside his shirt.

Features cold, expressionless, he faced her. "Go on in," he said in the same lifeless tone.

A long sigh escaped the girl's lips as frustration and a sense of helplessness flooded through her. She should have known it wouldn't be that easy, should have guessed he would be a step and a thought ahead of her. She was a fool to have made this attempt—she should have waited, laid an ambush as she'd planned on from the start.

Fingers tightening about the rawhide thong, she pressed down. The door swung in and she stepped through the opening. From a back corner of the half-dark room Luke's voice rising with relief greeted her.

"Zoe! By God but I'm glad to see you! Been wonder——"

His words trailed off as Rye moved in behind her and took up a position at the edge of the doorway. In the low-ceilinged room he seemed to tower above all else.

Ignoring the outlaw, the girl studied him for a long moment. Then, "If you're looking for the others, you're wasting your time," she said heavily.

At once Luke spoke up. "Walt and Curly—and the kid, ain't they with you?"

"No. I pulled out, left them flat. They ran Tom Horn off."

"You—you mean you're alone?" Braden continued in a strained voice. "Why, for hell's sake would you—?"

"They had something besides helping me—and you—on their minds," the girl replied with a shrug. Luke was chained to one of the logs making up the wall, she noted. The chinking had fallen away and Rye had looped the steel links around it.

The marshal had not moved, was still at the partly open doorway, staring out onto the slope below. It was evident he was not taking the girl at her word.

"Then you—" Luke began in a despairing voice.

"It's not over yet," Zoe cut in, determination coming again to the fore.

The lawman pivoted slowly, allowed the door to close. "You're wrong," he said flatly. "It's all over—for both of you."

Zoe met his hard gaze unflinchingly. "Don't bank on it, Marshal. Plenty can happen between here and that prison."

"Maybe, but you won't be around to see it," he said, and crossed to where Luke hunched in the corner. Reaching into a pocket of his vest, he produced a key, unlocked the cuffs encircling the outlaw's ankles.

"You plan to leave me here—chained to that log?" the girl asked sarcastically.

"I'll be handing you over to the nearest sheriff, have him lock you up for a few days," Rye answered, gathering in the leg irons. "Get up!"

Zoe stirred wearily as Braden pulled himself erect. His wrists were joined by a smaller chain connected to wide steel cuffs, she noted. Rye left nothing to chance.

"Now, maybe you will and maybe you won't," the outlaw said, regaining some of his cocksure confidence. "I got me a hunch Curly and Walt'll be showing up here before long. They ain't going to forget me." He frowned suddenly, shifted resentful eyes to the girl. "Goddammit, you should've stuck with them—not run off!"

She smiled wryly. "That would've been all right with you, wouldn't it?—their using me—"

"All I know is if they was here I'd be shucking these cuffs and figuring out a way to pay back this damned lawman for how he's been treating me!"

"Not likely," Rye said quietly. "Chances are they'd both be dead—and you along with them."

"Well, they're not the only ones," Zoe said, striving to break down some of the marshal's ironlike poise. "The deputy's looking for you, too. Says he's going to square up for something you did to him in Boston City."

Rye crossed to the door, opened it slightly and peered out. Braden stared at the girl.

"That's for true? Kirby's trailing him?"

If the news had registered on the lawman, he gave no indication of it. She nodded.

"We found out in Cimarron. Horn went there for some groceries. He heard about it then."

"Where'll he be?" Luke asked anxiously. "Was he ahead of you?"

"I don't know. He's somewheres along the trail, I guess."

Braden grinned broadly, glanced at Rye. "Like she said, Marshal, it's still a far piece to Yuma Prison—and you ain't got only Curly and Walt tracking you but you've got that loony deputy looking for a chance to gun you down, too. Besides that, there's Zoe here—"

"What shape's your horse in?" Rye said, turning to the girl.

Her small shoulders stirred indifferently. "Bad. I've been on the move day and night catching up—"

"You'd better hope he's got a few miles left in him," Rye snapped, reaching out for Braden. Grasping him by the arm, he pushed the outlaw toward the door. "We're moving out fast. You can either keep up or fall behind and join Luke's friends."

Zoe, a tightness gripping her, pushed past her husband and glanced out the door. Braden laughed.

"Told you, didn't I? Old Curly and Walt ain't about to forget me!"

"It's not them," Rye said, shoving him by the girl and into the open. "It's Pete Stanley and the others."

17

Rye had noticed the dust while he waited in the oak brush for Braden's wife to make her cautious approach to the door. And then later, standing inside the shack where he had left the outlaw when he went on to a nearby settlement, Galena Crossing, for supplies, he had watched four riders emerge in the hazy distance.

It could only be Stanley, and the last remaining members of his gang, Ollie King, Ben Polk and Amos Cook. They had not continued on to Silver City along the hogback trail, had instead discovered their error, doubled back and, as he had done with Braden, swung around the opposite side of the mountain. Somewhere along the way they had picked up the tracks left by the chestnut and Luke's black, and had followed them in; or perhaps they had spotted him coming from the settlement, as had Zoe Braden. He doubted they knew of the cabin—it had been a fortunate surprise to him—but once they caught sight of it they would conclude instantly the old structure was where he and Braden would be found.

"Mount up," he ordered tersely as Luke halted beside his horse.

He was giving the girl no thought, hoping she would elect to stay and join with Stanley. Having her tagging along on a spent horse could only slow him down.

"Who's Pete Stanley?" he heard her ask as he secured Luke's hands to the saddle.

Rye swore despairingly. It hadn't occurred to him, but Zoe could not have known about the outlaw's partners and their determination to kill Luke before he reached Yuma Prison. They would include her in that plan now, just as they did him, since both had become aware of their identities and, therefore, like Luke, must be silenced before they could talk. Leaving her behind was out of the question.

"Ask your husband," he said gruffly, freeing the outlaw's horse and his own.

Jaw set to angry lines, he swung onto the gelding, paused while the girl climbed onto her buckskin, and then, wheeling about, led the way to the rear of the cabin. There he cut onto a trail that angled upwards to the top of the bluffs. Looking down he could not see the four outlaws because of the brush, but they would be moving in, were probably somewhere near the mouth of the draw by that moment. Had he been wrong, they should be visible now on the long flat that lay between the hills and Galena Crossing.

"Marshal, listen here to me," Luke said as the horses, having gained the crest, strung out along the path. "Running like we're doing is plumb crazy! There's three of us now and we got plenty of guns. Let's just pull off here in the brush and when Pete and them comes along, we can open up on them."

Rye, ignoring the outlaw, looked again to the slopes below. The four men were still not in sight. A frown gathered on his forehead. They should be showing up. Could he have been wrong about them?

"Who is this Pete Stanley, Luke? You keep dodging the question."

There was impatience and a tone of disgust in the girl's voice, the lawman noted. Braden swore.

"Ain't dodging nothing, dammit! Him and them three jaspers are out to kill me—and if Rye don't do something about it, they're going to do it!"

"Why? I heard something about them back at that homesteader's where you stopped. You'd been shot, they said, by some friends. . . . None of it made any sense."

Luke swore again. "Ain't you got nothing in you but questions? We was friends once—sort of partners. Had a falling-out. Now they're sore at me."

Rye listened idly. Luke Braden was inclined to lie even when the truth was not only easier but much simpler and affected the situation not at all.

"But why would they want to kill you?" the girl persisted. "Must be more than just a falling-out."

"Oh, hell," the outlaw said heavily, finally facing up to it. "It was over a bank holdup. They're scared I'll talk, tell who they are. That satisfy you?"

"I suppose. Doesn't make much difference one way or another."

"Well, it ought! They're out to kill me—and I'm your husband. A real wife'd be plenty upset by—"

"Don't remind me of my past mistakes, Luke—and while we're talking about it, I want you to understand one thing. I told myself back in Boston City that because I was your wife it was up to me to help you all I could. I'll do that, but when it's over, one way or another, I'm through."

"You saying you're pulling out on me?"

"That's just what I mean."

Zoe was speaking as if he were not present, Rye realized, and making no bones about her intentions to help Luke if she could. Her determination had cooled, however. The Zoe Braden trailing wearily along behind her husband was a far different woman from the one who had declared herself so vehemently back in Boston City.

She'd finally gotten her fill of Luke, recognizing him for what he was, but, womanlike, she could not rid herself of the sense of loyalty and obligation the vows she had taken had instilled in her, as he had suspected. She was quite a girl, this Zoe Braden, he thought, and deserved better than a murdering, two-bit outlaw for a husband.

"Sure never figured you'd do this to me," Luke muttered. "Just ain't right. . . . Hell, you ain't even asked me if I was bad hurt from that shooting."

"I can see you're not—"

"Weren't no scratch! I bled like a stuck hog."

Braden's whining voice was beginning to grate on the lawman's nerves as they pressed steadily on. They were making poor time, however, slowed by Zoe's buckskin, and the miles he'd hoped to place between the outlaws and his party before any pursuit could get under way, were not to be. His best bet now was darkness, a couple of hours or so away—and Silver City.

It would be smart to keep going even after nightfall, get as close to the town as possible, where he could rid himself of the girl, before halting. There was only a remote chance of that; their horses were in almost as bad shape as Zoe's, the lawman realized.

The deputy . . . Linus Kirby. The girl had said he had joined the ranks of those who wanted to try their hand at cutting him down. Rye grinned tightly. Hell, Linus would have to get in line with all the others with a like ambition.

But he was the youngest so far—and the first lawman to make known his intentions. Rye guessed that made Kirby sort of special. He'd try and talk him out of it—something he'd ordinarily not bother to do—if they ever met face to face. Linus Kirby was nothing more than a kid who didn't know any better.

He should have taken that into consideration back in Boston City, he reckoned, when he'd laid one across the deputy's face. But hearing him bad-mouth Rufe Whitaker, who had long since forgotten more about being a good lawman than Kirby could ever learn, had rubbed him wrong. He'd try to pacify the boy if and when a showdown developed—hopefully never, but if it had to come, after he had delivered his prisoner to the warden at Yuma.

He had enough problems to contend with as it was. The four one-time partners of Braden who wanted him dead; Zoe, with her misplaced loyalty and sense of obligation and who could be expected to become a troublesome, even dangerous pest as she sought to help Luke escape; and possibly his two friends Hyde and Crow, who, contrary to the girl's belief, could still be on their trail.

He'd shortly change some of that, however. When they

reached Silver City he intended to break his usual rule and ride into town with his prisoner and the girl. Once there, he'd hand her over to the sheriff and have her held until he could get far enough along on the Yuma road to where there'd be no possibility of her catching up.

It was a strange feeling having her riding in company with him and his prisoner, knowing all the while she would take the first opportunity presented to free the man he had in custody. He would have to take precautions where Zoe was concerned, and, once they had halted for night camp, tie her up so that she could pose no problem. The same would hold true when they rode on in the morning. She wasn't taking kindly to thoughts of being locked in a jail, naturally, and if he gave her the chance she'd no doubt attempt to leave.

The cabin at the head of the draw was now far behind them, and, glancing back from time to time in search of riders or clouds of hanging dust that would indicate their presence on the trail, Rye had seen neither. Again he wondered if he'd been wrong about Stanley and the others, if he possibly was giving them too much credit for their abilities.

That they would have ridden to the cabin was a fairly certain conclusion, but there, finding no one present and failing also to note the tracks left by three horses slanting up the slope behind the shack for the top of the bluff, Pete Stanley could have decided he'd made a second mistake, and, returning to the flat, continued on to Galena Crossing.

It would be a stroke of good luck, if true, but as always John Rye would accept no probability, but only fact.

When he did not know for sure, it was his wont to expect the opposite, which, in this instance, was that the outlaws were still on his trail.

An hour after sunset, with the horses moving at snail's pace, heads slung low and legs trembling from fatigue, Rye called a halt in a secluded clearing a dozen yards off the trail and through which a small stream flowed briskly. Dismounting immediately, he pulled Luke Braden from the saddle, and with Zoe looking on coldly, chained him to a tree. He turned then to care for the three exhausted animals, staking them close to the water, where grass was plentiful.

Coming back into the center of the area, sack of grub and the necessary utensils for cooking in his hands, he paused to consider the girl. She had settled on a rotting log on the opposite side of the clearing from her husband, was dejectedly studying the toes of her boots. It wouldn't be necessary to bind her just yet, he decided. She was too tired to attempt an escape, and if she did manage somehow to get her buckskin saddled without his being aware of it, she'd not get far. The horse probably didn't have a short mile left in him.

Silent, he set the sacks down and began to collect wood for a fire. With full darkness rapidly closing in he need have no fear of smoke being seen, but he would keep the flames low so that no glare would reflect against the tops of the trees.

Zoe did not stir until he had begun the meal. She rose then, took over the chore of making coffee and doing whatever else needed attention. There was no conversation between her and Luke, or with Rye either. Weariness was having its restrictive effect upon them all and each sought only to appease hunger and then sleep.

They ate in a listless silence and before the food was gone Luke had dropped off and was snoring deeply. Zoe gathered up the utensils that required cleaning, carried them to the stream and scoured them with sand. When she returned Rye had stowed away his food stock, was spreading a blanket for her near the fire. He motioned for her to lie down. She shook her head.

"It's your blanket—you use it. I'll manage."

"Won't be needing it," he said gruffly, and, taking her by the arm, forced her onto the woolen cover.

Reaching then into a pocket, he produced two short lengths of rawhide cord. Pulling her feet together, he used one of the strips to link her ankles, taking care to place the knot at her heels, where she could not get at it. Without being ordered, Zoe then extended her arms, palms touching, fingers locked, to him for the thong to be wound about her wrists, all the while considering him with cool detachment.

The task completed, he took up a corner of the blanket and drew it over her.

"I'll keep the fire going," he said.

Zoe stirred indifferently. "Suit yourself."

Rye nodded crisply, and, crossing to where he had propped the shotgun against a tree, hung it under his arm and moved up into the thick brush above the clearing. Finding a place where he had an unobstructed view of the camp, he settled down, giving in at last to the weariness that dragged at him. A full night's rest was one thing he was in need of; he hoped nothing would occur to interrupt it.

Nothing did. Pete Stanley and his men made no appearance, nor did Crow and Curly Hyde, or the deputy, Linus Kirby, but with the breaking of first light Rye's face changed; Zoe Braden was gone.

18

The lawman, cursing himself for sleeping so soundly, walked quickly down into the clearing. Near the ashes of the fire he saw the rawhide thongs he'd used to tie the girl's wrists and ankles. There were several scorched and blackened pieces. She had apparently waited until he was asleep, managed to drag a coal or a burning brand from the fire and burned the strip binding her wrists in two. Removing the cord about her ankles had then been easy.

With Luke watching him in silence, a broad grin on his lips, Rye glanced toward the horses. The buckskin, of course, was gone. The lawman swore again; if he'd roused only once to replenish the fire, as he'd planned, he could have stopped her.

"Fooled you good, didn't she, Marshal?" Braden said in a gleeful sort of way. "She's a pistol, that Zoe!"

Rye merely shook his head, and, gathering in some of the wood he'd brought in the night before, started a fire and set water to heating for coffee.

"You can be looking for her to be waiting for you somewheres along the trail," the outlaw continued. "She won't quit 'til she's got me scot-free."

The lawman began to slice bacon into the frying pan. He couldn't care less about Zoe Braden, he assured himself; he hadn't wanted her along in the first place and had permitted it only because there'd been no choice. Actually, in so doing he'd broken his own rules—perhaps even gone a little soft. But it was all behind him now. The girl was no longer his problem.

The meal was over quickly and the fire hurriedly extinguished to eliminate as much smoke as possible. When they were loaded and ready to move out and Rye was cuffing Braden to the saddle, the outlaw looked out across the hills and frowned.

"We be going to Silver City now?"

"No."

There was no need. He had planned to do so in order to rid himself of the girl. In taking her leave she had made the trip unnecessary.

"That mean we're heading straight across for Arizona?"

Rye, swinging onto the chestnut, nodded as he brought the big horse about and gathered in the lead rope attached to the outlaw's black. He considered Luke with faint amusement.

"It make a difference to you which way we go to reach Yuma Prison?"

"Ain't that—I was thinking about Zoe. She'll figure we'll go south, not west."

No weapon, no grub, a stranger in a country where settlements were few and marauding Apaches were only too plentiful, Zoe Braden would be facing serious problems. But they were of her own making and could not become his.

"Sure could get bad for her," Luke said. All his earlier gloating satisfaction at her escape had evaporated.

"It's a hard life," Rye said laconically, and, brushing the chestnut with his spurs, rode out of the clearing.

The girl could be observing their movements from a safe distance, the lawman realized after a time—not that it changed anything. It was just that if she hung around them there was less chance of her getting herself lost. Had she struck out on her own for Silver City or gone in search for some other settlement with the intention of buying a weapon and a supply of grub, she very easily could go astray in the multitude of canyons and slopes that all looked the same to the unpracticed eye.

The second possibility that occurred to him was more comforting: it could be that he had seen the last of her. She could be giving up the idea of aiding Luke to escape. That he meant nothing to her and that she intended to have nothing more to do with him even if she enabled him to gain his freedom, had been made clear. Her failure to aid him back at the cabin had been decisive; maybe she would now forget it and go home.

He hoped so. Zoe Braden would never see the moment when she could take Luke away from him and set him free, for if such time ever came, he would be compelled to look upon her as neither man nor woman but a threat, and act accordingly.

At the bottom of the slope Rye stayed close to the thick brush that fringed its edge. He had a wide, panoramic view of the country to their rear at that point, and, gaining a slight rise, he halted, had a lengthy, searching look at the rolling hills and flats. He saw no movement that could mark the presence of Pete Stanley and his crowd, or of anyone else, and, satisfied, resumed his course.

On due west lay the sprawling San Augustine Plains,

and he must skirt that wide open stretch of land upon which a rider would be visible for miles. He'd swing down through the ragged San Mateo Mountains to the towering Black Range, and, using two-mile-high Mogollon Peak as a landmark, cross over into Arizona.

From there he'd cut south to the San Simon Valley country, and there, if he encountered no trouble, strike west for Arizona City, or Yuma, as some were calling the settlement. The prison itself was close by, perched on a hill that overlooked the Colorado River, and once there the job would be finished. He'd take a few days off, maybe go on down into Mexico and lay around for a while.

But that was time and many miles into the future. He still had Pete Stanley at his heels—and there was that pair who had started out with Zoe Braden, not to mention Linus Kirby and the Apaches that roamed the Arizona hills and deserts preying on small parties and solitary pilgrims. The journey was a long way from being over and he reckoned he'd best not think that far ahead.

They made camp that night in a high country valley. Pine and fir trees grew thickly on the slopes, while along the fast-running creek that carved a path along its floor there were many cottonwoods, leaves shivering ceaselessly in the cool breeze, prickly clumps of wild gooseberries, slender willows and other shrubs.

The night, a comfortable one, passed without incident and they were up and on their way shortly after first light that next morning. Rye was gradually becoming more convinced that he had not only shaken Stanley and his outlaw partners as well as Crow and Curly Hyde, if, indeed, they had been in the offing, but also Zoe Braden.

There had been smoke riding in the sky to the west that previous day, designating the location of a settlement or a ranch, and very likely she had made her way to it.

Sunset found them in the Black Range, and after another uneventful night, they were again on the move with cloud-piercing Baldy Peak now clearly visible in the west. They made a dry camp in its shadow, and when the sun dropped behind Arizona's Gila Mountains at the close of the following day they had crossed the border and were halting along a small river Rye recalled was named the San Francisco.

He waited until full dark to build the fire they needed for cooking, and when finished with it, quickly stamped it out. Such brought immediate complaints from the outlaw, who was feeling the night's sharp chill. The lawman shook his head.

"Too risky. This is Apache country—will be until we're pretty close to Yuma."

"Been plenty of other folks traveling across here—"

"Most of them stick to the main roads, where they'll have company. Some protection that way."

"Then why ain't we doing it?"

"You can blame your friend Stanley and his crowd, and maybe those other two jaspers that think they're going to take you away from me."

Braden mumbled, jerked at the chain linking him to a thick-trunked mesquite. "Hell of a note. . . . We ain't seen no sign of Indians."

"They're out there. Chances are we've already been spotted."

The outlaw glanced about nervously, his bearded

features in a tight frown. "I'd as soon see Pete and them show up as a bunch of murdering redskins—"

"You're dead either way," the lawman said bluntly.

Out of the high mountains of New Mexico, traveling was easier and that next day they made excellent time, coming to a stop at nightfall in the Gila Mountains, which, only hours before, had been but a blue, hazy outline in the far distance. Again John Rye took care to draw no attention to their presence—a precaution that paid off well late the following morning.

They were moving down a narrow arroyo, angling toward another range of hills, when motion off to their left caught his attention. Instantly he swung into the thick brush at the edge of the sandy wash, finger placed to his lips as a warning for silence to Braden.

A scant quarter mile away, riding a course paralleling their own, was a party of five braves. Lean, dusky men, their half-naked bodies shone dully in the harsh sunlight. From the direction they were coming, Rye judged they had passed close by the area where he and Luke Braden had spent the night.

When they had disappeared beyond the clumps of rabbit bush and multi-trunked mesquite, the marshal bucked his head at the outlaw.

"That enough proof?" he demanded, grimly.

Braden made no reply, but as they rode on he began to glance continually from side to side as well as to their back trail, apparently expecting more Apaches to show. That he was now convinced that Rye's precautions were wise and necessary was evident.

Camp that night was a small hollow, well up on the

slope of a hill where brush shielded them from possible searching eyes passing below.

"No fire," Rye said as he passed out the food they would eat in lieu of a regular meal. "Could be that bunch of braves would smell the smoke if the wind changed. Have to do without coffee."

Braden grunted a reply. Then, "We going to have to keep on doing it this way—no fire and no decent eating— clean to Yuma?"

"Just about. Be some safer once we're the other side of the Maricopas."

"Maricopas—what's that?"

"Mountains. They're about halfway between here and where we're headed. Ought to—"

The faint hammer of hooves brought the lawman's words to a stop. He drew himself partly erect, features taut, and looked down into the arroyo below.

"Who is it?" Luke asked in a hushed voice. "Them Apaches again?"

Rye motioned to him for silence, continued to watch the wash as the pounding of hooves grew louder. Suddenly yells broke out. A horse, barely distinguishable in the half dark, flashed by, heading up the arroyo. Only a length or so behind it appeared a second horse—and then another. Even in the dim visibility it was easy to recognize the latter two riders and understand what was taking place; Apaches in pursuit of some luckless pilgrim.

A woman's scream suddenly pierced the hush. John Rye, settling back, stiffened, again threw his attention to the wash. The thud of hooves was audible once more,

this time a measured, slow beat. The braves were returning with their captive.

"That yelling—sounded like Zoe!" Braden said in a
hoarse whisper.

The same thought had come to the lawman, pricking
at his conscience with growing insistence. . . . The horses
came into view, those of the Apaches on either side of
their prisoner. Rye strained to make out the color of the
animal, the identity of its rider. A gust of irritation swept
him. He could tell little about the figure cowering on the
saddle, but the horse was Zoe Braden's buckskin.

19

Rye swore deeply. Damn the fool girl, anyway! She'd let herself fall into the hands of the Apaches—probably the same bunch of five they'd seen earlier. He ought to just forget it, let her work her way out of the trouble she was now in on her own. He'd just about decided she was gone, no longer someone to worry about; instead, she'd blundered into a party of renegade braves and it wasn't hard to envision what lay ahead for her.

"It was Zoe—wasn't it?"

The lawman, battling himself over the question of whether to make an attempt to rescue the girl or stick strictly to his own business, as was his hard-and-fast rule, nodded slowly. Leaving Braden unguarded, even if securely chained, with Pete Stanley and his gang, and the possibility of Hyde and Walt Crow also in the area carrying on a search for him, went against everything John Rye believed was sensible and constituted the performance of his duty. But the girl had to be helped.

"You're aiming to go after her, ain't you?"

The hoofbeats had faded. Like as not the Indians were halted for the night somewhere on down the arroyo. Rye stirred angrily.

"Ought to forget it!" he snapped impatiently. "But I can't."

Wheeling, he crossed to where Braden lay, made a close examination of the leg chain and cuffs, turned then toward the horses.

"You leaving me here? My God, Marshal—give me a gun so's I can protect myself. Them redskins could be all around us."

"Stay quiet—that's all you need to do," Rye said, pausing to remove his spurs.

"But—but supposing you don't come back—"

"I'll be back," the lawman replied, and, bridling the chestnut, heaved himself onto its back and rode down to the floor of the arroyo.

He rode slowly, listening intently into the night. Somewhere farther on he could hear shouts, laughter. The sounds seemed to come from a point near a jutting bit of land that extended, butte-like from the mountain. He halted. There was no need for the chestnut; the Indians had made their camp no more than a half mile distant. Sliding off the horse, he led him into the nearby brush, anchored him to a stout bush. Turning quickly, he started down the sandy wash at a quiet trot.

The glare of a fire warned him when he was near the camp. Cutting back up to the slope and out of the arroyo, he crouched low and began to work his way toward the flickering glow. He'd heard no more yelling or laughing, reckoned the braves were eating and not quiet for any other reason.

Relief stirred him as he drew nearer. Voices now came to him; low, guttural conversation. Zoe was evidently being ignored while they hashed over some topic or were engaged in filling their bellies. Down flat, Rye wormed in closer until he was in the brush that encircled a small clearing.

There were five braves—and they were eating. Squatting on their haunches around the fire, each had a piece of meat, a portion of some small animal, evidently a rabbit, they'd roasted over the flames. A second was still suspended by a curved stick in the heat, waiting to be consumed. The portions they held were still hot and the men were continually tossing the bits from hand to hand as they sought to cool the meat enough to eat. He could not see Zoe.

Drawing back carefully, Rye changed position, crawled in to the camp at a point several yards to his left. He saw the girl then. She was directly below him. Her hands were tied behind her and a rawhide rope encircling her waist and neck bound her to the trunk of a tree. She was watching the braves, her features pale in the flickering orange light of the fire.

Farther over, the vague outlines of the horses could be seen in a thicket of brush. That the Apaches intended to spend the night there was apparent, else they would not have hobbled their mounts.

Rye, ignoring his holstered gun, drew his knife and slipped silently toward the girl. He came up to her from behind, thus keeping her between himself and the braves, some thirty feet away. She did not hear him and when he reached her, he put his head close to hers.

"Don't move," he murmured.

Startled, Zoe jerked slightly, but no sound escaped her lips. The lawman laid the sharp edge of his knife against the braided rawhide, sawed through it, eyes all the while on the Apaches. They were finishing up the first rabbit, were now tearing the second one apart, smacking and licking their fingers as they divided the pieces. One paused to glance over his shoulder at the girl. When he turned back to the others he said something and all laughed.

"Got to do this quiet," he said, his low voice tense, sharp, and betraying the angry impatience he still felt at being forced to jeopardize his prisoner for her sake. "Pull away from the tree, then start hitching your way back to me. The brush will hide you."

She nodded her understanding. Rye saw her shoulders dip forward and to the side, and then she was inching toward him. There was no time to spare; Zoe would be realizing that. Once the last rabbit was eaten they would turn their attention to her. When she was clear of the tree, he slipped his arm around her waist, drew her back into the deep shadows.

"The horses," he murmured, coming upright. "I'll have to stampede them—else they'll start hunting us."

Turning, he ducked back into the brush, and, with Zoe following silently at his heels, made the short circle to where the buckskin and the Apaches' ponies were waiting. He wasted no time glancing at the braves, seeing if they were yet occupied with their meal; the instant any one of them finished and looked to their captive, the alarm would go up.

Slashing the buckskin's hobbles, he handed the reins to the girl and pointed toward the arroyo. "Head up that way. Lead your horse. I'll catch up."

Zoe began to drop back toward the wash, with the

buckskin trailing tiredly behind her. Rye waited until she had gained the sandy-floored cleft and then turned his attention to the Apaches' horses. It was important the animals be scattered, claim the attention of the braves; otherwise escape from them would be difficult.

Moving among them hurriedly, he sliced through their rope restraints, started them drifting off into the brush in a direction opposite to that taken by Zoe. The animals were skittish, reacted quickly, and that was good. He wanted to avoid any gunshots if at all possible; such would be heard for a considerable distance and could draw the attention of Pete Stanley and others, bring them in to investigate the source.

Using his weapon to frighten the Apache ponies wouldn't be necessary, however, he saw with relief. All were hastily disappearing into the night. He turned to go, follow the girl. In that same instant a shout went up from the Indian camp. They had discovered their prisoner was missing.

Drawing his pistol, a taut grin on his lips, Rye moved off through the brush. There was still time to get past the camp, reach the arroyo—if his luck held.

A slim, dark shape loomed up before him. He swore wryly at his own foolish optimism, and as the brave lunged at him, knife glinting in an upraised hand, he struck out with his pistol. The heavy weapon struck the Apache on the side of the head, driving him to his knees.

A stride to the left a rifle blasted through the night, its orange flash all but blinding the lawman. He pivoted, fired instinctively, heard the brave grunt as the bullet smashed into him. Another shadow drifted out of the

The Doomsday Marshal

brush close by. Rye triggered his weapon again, and bent low, rushed on, uncertain whether he'd hit his target or not.

He reached the wash and slowed. There were no sounds of the remaining braves following. He looked ahead. Zoe and the buckskin were dim outlines a short distance on. Running hard, he hurriedly overtook her, and, boosting her onto the saddle, swung up behind her and put the buckskin to a laboring trot.

They reached the brush where he'd left the chestnut, and, dropping to the ground, he pointed up the slope.

"Camp's there—stay mounted!"

Zoe spurred the buckskin by him, and, freeing his horse, he sprang onto its back and followed her to the small clearing. Luke Braden greeted them with a heavy sigh.

"I heard them gunshots. I was worried—"

Rye scarcely heard the outlaw. He was hastily collecting gear and making ready to move on. When all was set he released the outlaw, locked him to his saddle and climbing back onto the chestnut, headed on up the slope. Zoe pressed in close to him.

"Marshal, I want to thank—"

"Forget it!" he snapped. "We've got to get the hell out of here—fast!"

20

They followed no trail but slanted across the slope, moving as quietly as possible. No words passed between them, both Zoe and Luke realizing the danger all were in and caught up by the urgency pressing the big lawman, devoting their efforts solely to flight.

At first they could hear an occasional shout below in the arroyo as the Apaches searched for their scattered horses, but as they worked their way steadily off into the opposite direction and the wall of trees and brush separating them from the Apache camp grew in depth, the sounds gradually faded.

After a time they broke out onto the crest of the slope, and with the dark, starlit sky hanging low over them, Rye drew to a halt deep in the tall pines. He dismounted at once, strode directly to Zoe Braden. There was a grimness to him as he all but dragged the girl from her horse and made a thorough search of her person. When he was finished she shook her head angrily.

"Would have told you I didn't have a gun—if you'd asked."

He paused, looked at her, his chiseled features cold in the pale light. "What makes you think I'd take your word for it?" he snapped, and turned back to the chestnut. "Don't unsaddle. We'll be moving on at daylight."

Braden rattled the chain of his cuffs. "How about letting me get off this here nag—?"

Rye produced the key, opened one of the steel wrist bands. When the outlaw had come to the ground, he pushed him to one of the smaller pines, attached the leg irons and restored the handcuff.

Luke put his attention on Zoe as the lawman moved away. "You see anything of Curly and Walt?"

"No," the girl replied, sinking wearily onto a log. "Those other men, either."

"You been hanging around, trailing us?"

"No," Zoe said again. "Lost you when I went to that town—one somewheres west of here. Thought you were ahead of me and I was trying to catch up when those Indians saw me." She hesitated, glanced at Rye resting against one of the many large pines. "Still want to thank you—"

"I don't want your thanks," he said harshly. "Just want you to keep out of my way. . . . You get yourself in a fix like that again and I won't bother."

Zoe looked down, shoulders stirring faintly. Luke Braden hawked, spat. "How's it happen you didn't just shoot up them redskins, Marshal—all of them? We wouldn't have to be running from them right now if you had of."

"Not them I'm thinking about. It's your friends. I was hoping not to use a gun at all. They're bound to have heard the shooting."

"Yeh, expect they did. . . . How many of them devils did you kill?"

"One, maybe two," Rye said, disinterestedly.

"Can't figure where Curly and Walt are," the outlaw continued, turning back to Zoe. "Ought've showed up before now. You do any looking for them?"

"No."

"Well, why the hell didn't you? You ain't going to be much help to me, way you're doing. When you was in that town, why didn't you buy a gun?"

"It was either spend what money I had on a second-hand pistol or go hungry. Decided I'd rather have some food."

Luke swore in disgust. "Seems you ain't so keen on helping me as you claim."

"I'm here," Zoe said. "That ought to prove something. I could have just stayed in that town—"

From across the way John Rye's voice, irritable and impatient, cut into her words. "Do your quarreling tomorrow. I want it quiet while we're here."

"We keeping you from sleeping, Marshal?" Braden asked, grinning.

"Worry about those Apaches, and your friend Pete Stanley—not me," Rye said. "They're around here somewhere. That talking you're doing will make it easy for them to find us."

There was no more conversation after that, and, fighting the heaviness that weighted his eyes for another few minutes, the lawman saw that both Zoe and Luke had dropped off to sleep, and settled back to also get some rest.

He was up at first light. Arousing the girl and his prisoner, he got them mounted, and, making no explanations, led off down the mountainside. They would halt for a meal once they were in the valley below; the presence of the Apaches in the general area still troubled him, for with daylight he knew they would begin a search for the girl and the man who had slain one or possibly two of their party while freeing her and scattering their horses. Contrary to what he had told the Bradens earlier, he doubted they had made any serious effort during the night; darkness restricted the activities of a red man just as it did a white.

Two hours later, with Luke grumbling constantly, Rye pulled off into a narrow side canyon on the opposite slope to the one they had descended, and, after releasing the outlaw and chaining him in the usual fashion to a tree, he began to prepare a meal.

He paid no attention to Zoe, assuming an uncaring attitude that made it clear it mattered little whether she remained or went her way. But the girl was not inclined to stand idly by, and unasked she took over the cooking chore once he had the food items laid out and the fire going, leaving him to care for the horses.

It was a good meal, Rye had to admit as he ate his share of the bacon, potatoes and onions all fried to a crisp brown. The coffee lacked the strength he preferred and to remedy that he added another handful of crushed beans to the pot, which drew only a shrug from Zoe.

"How far to Yuma?" Braden asked from his place beside the tree.

"Six, maybe seven days."

The outlaw stared out over the ragged hills and long flat. "It all country like this?"

"About half of it."

"Three days more of rough riding," Luke said, groaning. "Hell, chained to that damned saddle, going up and down them hills—you could at least forget hooking me to the horn so's I could straighten up now and then."

"No chance," the lawman said flatly.

"Why not? Sure can't get away—not with you carrying that scatter-gun. Could cut me in two with it before I got ten feet. . . . I'd give you my word—"

"Your word's worth nothing to me, and, far as shooting you, it'll never happen unless you force me into it. I aim to get you to Yuma Prison alive—if I can."

Zoe took a swallow of coffee, grimaced. "Is it true that you've never lost a prisoner?"

Rye nodded. Luke extended his cup to her for a refill, laughing.

"Maybe so, but they ain't always breathing when he gets there with them! Ain't that the truth, Marshal?"

"The truth," the lawman replied with no particular heat. "It's up to the prisoner."

Zoe shuddered. "It must be a terrible thing, always being on your guard, expecting the worst—and ready to kill or be killed."

He regarded her with indifference. "You learn to live with it."

"But it changes you, makes you cold and hard—and an outsider around other folks. Doesn't that bother you?"

"Man wearing a badge usually is an outsider, as you call it. People want the law but they resent the man who has to enforce it."

"Yeh, about the only friend a lawman's got is another lawman," Luke said, "and I reckon there's even a-plenty

of them that ain't got no use for Mister Rye. That right,
Marshal?"

It was, the lawman admitted to himself. There were
many who disliked him because of the far-reaching authority his special commission afforded him. Such had
disturbed him somewhat at first, but like all other dis-
agreeable and unavoidable facts of life, he'd gotten
used to it.

"Whatever you say, Luke," he murmured.

The outlaw grinned. "Sure must be hell not having no
friends! Take me now, I got plenty of them—strung out
clean across the country. Good ones, too."

"Yeh, real good ones," Rye said dryly. "I can think of
four who like you so much they want you dead."

"Aw, Pete and them are just scared. I'm talking about
the ones like Walt Crow and Curly Hyde." Luke paused,
glared at Zoe. "If it hadn't been for her, you'd a heard
from them a long time ago!"

The lawman leaned forward, poured himself another
cup of coffee. He was not overlooking the men mentioned
by Braden but to him they represented a far less serious
threat than did Pete Stanley and his followers. Their interest lay in aiding Luke Braden to escape and to do so
they would have to go up against him; Stanley and his
crowd wanted Braden dead, and to accomplish that they
needed only to get within rifle range.

That he had managed to shake them back at the old
cabin near Galena Crossing seemed fairly certain now,
but he had not seen the last of them; they had everything to lose if Braden and he—and Zoe, too, reached
Yuma Prison alive. He gave a moment's thought as to

where they might be, where they could have gone after losing the trail. If they knew the country, they likely had hurried on ahead and would be waiting somewhere this side of Yuma. There was but one road across the desert after a man left the town of Arroyo Seco, a distance of a hundred miles at least, and making the crossing without being seen would be impossible. He should start thinking about that long, lonely stretch of desolation, come up with some sort of plan to avoid it before they reached the settlement.

"Marshal, I've been meaning to ask you—how many men've you killed?"

Luke's question was one no man would ordinarily ask another but he was taking enjoyment from taunting the lawman, knowing there was no likelihood of Rye turning on him. The marshal was silent for a long minute.

"Just the ones that forced me to do it," he said quietly, and, emptying his cup into the fire, got to his feet, and began to collect the utensils they'd used for the meal. There was no stream nearby and all would have to go without cleaning until later.

Zoe arose, gave him her help and shortly they were ready to move out again. Rye, glancing about to be certain nothing was being overlooked, crossed to where Luke sat. Key in hand, he released the leg cuffs and gathered up the chain.

"Let's go," he said, and stepped back.

Braden drew himself erect, stretched, yawned. "Asking you again if you'll—"

"No," the lawman said before he could finish. "Get on your horse."

Shrugging, Luke started across the small clearing. Zoe, waiting beside the buckskin, thrust a foot into the stirrup, started to mount. In a single, flowing motion Braden seized her by the arm, whirled her about and threw her into John Rye.

The lawman, never completely off guard, caught the girl with his left hand, swung the leg chain he was holding with the other. The steel links struck the outlaw behind the ear, knocking him to the ground. Rye, lips set to a hard line, moved toward him—he froze as a voice came from the nearby brush.

"Stand easy, Marshal. We got you covered from both sides."

21

Rye, his features bleak, stiffened slowly. From the corner of an eye he saw Zoe pull back in fear while in front of him, blood trickling down the side of his head, Luke Braden pulled himself unsteadily to his feet. He came half about, stared at the man moving in from the fringe of brush—a short, dark individual with black curly hair and beard. He could only be the one called Hyde.

"Where the goddam hell you been?" Braden demanded.

Curly, pistol leveled at Rye, grinned. "Tracking you, that's where. Them gunshots last night finally done it for us. . . . Come on in, Walt. The marshal's tame as a little puppy dog."

Crow, a bit older and larger than his partner and with narrow, smirking features, stepped from behind a large pine. He was not smiling, and he had his eyes on Zoe.

"Sure glad to see you, Walt," Luke said, "both of you. Was beginning to worry a mite."

"That woman of yours set us afoot," Crow replied. "Lost dang nigh a day catching up our horses. Wouldn't be here now if it wasn't for Curly's tracking—and her."

"Her?" Braden echoed, puzzled.

"Yeh, her," Crow said, and moving up to Rye took his pistol from its holster, thrust it under his waistband.

"What's she got to do with it?"

"Me and Curly's got a little unfinished business with her. . . . Stand over yonder, Marshal."

Rye moved slowly across the open ground to where he alone faced the men. His expression had not changed and his eyes seemed to have recessed beneath his thick brows and taken on a definite coldness.

"Get the key off'n him, take these goddam cuffs off me," Braden ordered, motioning to Curly. "Just about rubbed me raw."

John Rye shook his head slowly. "Don't do it. I'm warning you now—you're interfering with the law. Means the pen for you if you turn him loose."

Hyde had not moved. "We ain't caring nothing about him, Marshal."

Luke Braden came about sharply. "What's that mean?"

"Means me and Walt don't give one damn what he does with you—"

"What?" the outlaw yelled incredulously. "It was what you come here for, wasn't it—to help me?"

"Reckon maybe that's how it was at first—leastwise that was part of it. Then being around your woman all the time we plumb forgot about you. Hell, Luke, you're going to swing, anyways. If this here marshal don't get you to Yuma, some other'n will."

"We've always had us a powerful wanting for her," Crow added, nodding at Zoe. "What we're aiming to do is take her with us."

"You won't be taking me anywhere!" the girl snapped. "I'll see you in hell first."

"Maybe, but not right off, lady," Hyde said quietly. "We

been thinking about you since way back in Boston City, only you was so high-toney you'd hardly even looked at us. Then when you talked us into this here deal of helping Luke we figured things'd changed and we was going to be good friends after all."

"Didn't work that way a'tall," Crow said. "She hadn't changed—not one danged bit. Even put us off with that gun she's carrying."

"That there gun!" Hyde exclaimed suddenly. "I sure forgot all about it. You best take it off her, Walt, else she'll be trying to use it again. It'll be in her pocket."

Zoe flicked Rye with a glance, faced Crow. "I don't have it—I lost it back on the trail."

Crow grunted, patted the pockets of her trousers and jacket, taking care to do so thoroughly, and stepped away.

"Reckon she did lose it."

Hyde rubbed at his jaw with his free hand, nodded. "Well, anyways we—"

"What the goddam hell's all this yammering for?" Luke Braden demanded in an exasperated voice. "You come to help me; now you're talking about my wife and how you been wanting her. All right, take her. You got us both. All I'm saying is, unlock these here handcuffs."

"Just it, Luke, we ain't wanting you—and we ain't honing to get ourselves crosswise with the law unless we just have to. . . . Marshal, all we want's the woman, and we're ready to make a deal with you."

Rye felt the girl's eyes pressing him. He glanced at her. There was a hopelessness in them as if she knew it mattered little to him what became of her, that fulfilling his obligation to the oath he'd sworn was all that counted.

"I don't make deals—"

"Maybe you'd best this time. We got you by the short hair and these here guns Walt and me are holding says we can do what we please—but we ain't dumb enough to get in trouble with the law unless we have to."

"Curly—goddammit, you can't—"

"Shut up, Luke," Crow said in a hard voice. "You ain't got nothing to do with this."

"The hell I ain't! I'm why you're here—"

"Not any more," Crow said softly. "She's the reason now."

"Then go ahead and take her. I give her to you. All I'm asking is that you turn me loose so's I can head out of here—"

"What I'm trying to say, Marshal," Hyde continued, ignoring Braden, "is, you give us the woman and we'll ride on. You keep your prisoner and we won't never bother you again."

Rye studied the man coldly. Zoe Braden was a handicap and a hindrance, and turning her over to the two men would relieve him of having to be forever on the alert for an attempt on her part to free Luke. With her gone and along with her Walt Crow and Curly Hyde, he'd need only to concentrate on getting past Pete Stanley and the men siding him. It was the logical way to solve a serious problem but somehow John Rye was finding the solution, which would be in accord with his straight-down-the-middle way of performing his duty, hard to accept.

"What if I turn you down?"

"Well then, we'll just have to take her, I reckon. We've got big plans for her, being the looker she is, when we're done."

"Means you'll have to shoot me. Braden, too."

"Know that—reason we're trying to talk sense to you. Done said we ain't anxious to get slanchwise with the law, but if we have to, we have to. We figure it'll be worth it."

"One damned woman worth all that?" Braden said in disgust. "Turn me loose and I'll find you a dozen like her —better even. A half a dozen apiece if you want them."

"We're wanting her," Crow said in a dogged voice. "Got a lot of making up to do for them highfaluting airs she was putting on back in Boston City—and on the trail."

"What about it, Marshal?" Hyde asked, coming again to the question. "Expect you'd like to get shed of her and I know you sure don't want to spoil that there record of your'n."

Rye folded his arms across his chest, said nothing. Abruptly Walt Crow swore, reached out, seized Zoe by the wrist.

"Hell, he ain't going to do it, Curly. You take care of them while I see to the lady—"

"Get away from him!" the lawman shouted at the girl, and darted a hand inside his shirt for the pistol he'd taken from Zoe Braden back at the cabin.

Throwing himself to the ground, Rye fired point-blank at Curly. Hyde, weapon out and leveled, staggered as the bullet drove into him and began to fall. In that same moment Crow wheeled as the girl wrenched free, making a stab for his gun. Rye fired again. Walt Crow jolted, a frown on his narrow features, sank to his knees, weapon dangling from nerveless fingers. Braden lunged toward it.

Instantly the marshal's gun covered the outlaw. "One more step," he said in a grating, remote way, "and you're dead as they are."

Braden caught himself, raised his manacled hands, palms forward. "I ain't doing nothing—"

"Get back against that tree," Rye ordered, and pulled himself to his feet.

When Luke had complied, the lawman moved through the thin layers of drifting powder smoke to where Crow lay. Still utterly self-controlled and coldly efficient, he rolled the body over, recovered the pistol that had been taken from him. Going a step further, he picked up the weapons the two men were carrying, threw them off into the brush. Coming about, he then laid his flat, emotionless gaze on Zoe and the outlaw.

"Get mounted—"

The girl turned hurriedly to her buckskin. Braden, quickly recovered and swaggering a little, climbed onto his horse.

"They're dead—what's the hurry?"

"Apaches," Rye said bluntly as he chained the outlaw to his saddle.

He wheeled at once to the chestnut, swung aboard and again placed his attention on Zoe. "Lead off," he said, pointing at a distant peak. "Head for that mountain."

22

Zoe spurred out of the clearing at once, throwing a quick glance at the bodies of Walt Crow and Curly Hyde, and curved down into a narrow wash. Rye motioned Luke Braden to fall in behind her, forgoing the lead rope to the black for the time being.

As he'd feared, the braves were on their trail almost immediately—four lean shapes hunched low on their ponies and streaming down the slope at a reckless pace. Seeing them, Rye shouted a warning at the girl and Braden. Both looked back briefly and then increased their speed.

They reached the edge of the hills, raced out onto a long flat, barren except for snakeweed, yucca and an occasional cluster of restless ocotillo. At once the horses began to lengthen their stride and gain on the Apache ponies as the near level ground offered smoother footing.

A gunshot echoed faintly, followed by several more as the braves, realizing they were being outdistanced, opened up with their rifles. The bullets fell short and when the lawman glanced back as they reached a wide arroyo along which mesquite and paloverde broke the sameness of the flat, the Apaches had pulled off and were circling back toward the hills.

Rye shouted the word to Zoe and Luke. Both slowed

their heaving horses to a walk and he drew up alongside them. The lawman felt the girl's eyes upon him searching, probing. He nodded and a small smile of relief parted her lips.

"Sure hope that's the last we'll see of them savages," Braden said, brushing the sweat from his face with a forearm.

"It will be," the marshal replied.

"Yeh, reckon they're going back there to do some scalping—"

"Doubt that. All they'll be interested in is their guns and horses."

Rye was speaking in his usual sparse way, the brittle tension that had possessed him back in the clearing now dissipated and a part of the past.

Braden again bent forward, swiped at the sweat on his face. "Poor old Walt and Curly—you sure didn't give them much of a chance, Marshal."

The lawman's shoulders twitched. "I'm no hand at giving anybody a free shot at me," he said dryly.

"Kind of think maybe you enjoyed it—"

"Your right to think what you want—but I don't like killing. Never have. Just that sometimes you can't avoid it."

"You didn't have a choice back there," Zoe said, coming into the conversation. "Hyde was going to—"

"Keep your lip out of this!" Braden shouted, breaking into her words. "It's your fault things turned out how they did! If you'd done things right—got along with them—"

"Let them do what they wanted with me, that what you mean?"

"Why not? What'd be the difference? I sure wasn't the first man you ever had, and you can bet I won't be the last, neither. What did you draw the line on them for? If you'd played your cards right like you was supposed to, I'd be loose right now—and they'd be alive."

Zoe glanced at Rye. "I doubt it."

"Well, you just keep on doubting!" Luke shouted angrily. "You're thinking the marshal there's mighty big potatoes. He's just another man, that's all—and a real tricky one. . . . Goddam you, Zoe—you're siding in with him! If I could get loose, lay my hands on you, I'd—"

"Ease off," Rye cut in sharply. The outlaw's constant bickering had long since grown old.

Luke shifted on his saddle, swore again. After a few moments he said, "Just can't forget how you blasted them boys—didn't even hardly bat an eye."

"They forced the play," the lawman replied, a thread of anger now in his tone. "Said before I don't hold with killing a man—outlaw or not—but when it has to be done I'll not back down from doing it. . . . While you're bleeding over them you might think about that woman and her boys that you shot down—and those two men you hacked to death with a sickle—"

"They got in my way."

"That an excuse or a reason?"

Braden's shoulders lifted, fell. "Don't want to talk about it," he mumbled lamely.

"Goes for Crow and Curly Hyde," Rye said quietly. "I don't want to hear any more about them."

They rode on, crossing a hot, dry land. Sometime after noon they forded the San Pedro River, flowing low and crystal clear in the driving sunlight. They rested there for an hour and then pressed on, and when darkness began to close in they found themselves in the Tortolita Hills and halted for the night.

At daylight they resumed the journey, conscious of the steadily increasing heat as they bore for the murky, blue shadowed range of mountains in the distance that Rye called the Maricopas.

"How far'll they be from Yuma?" Braden asked, repeating a question he'd voiced at various times previous.

"Hundred miles, a bit more."

"It country like this?"

"Desert. Be hot but won't be at its worst at this time of the year. Couple of months from now it'll be different. Have to cross it at night, or not at all then."

"How long will it take us?" Zoe wondered. She had removed her jacket and unbuttoned the collar of her shirt. Small patches of sweat showed on her cheeks and the folds of her dark hair looked damp.

John Rye's thoughts turned to the girl. He had given little consideration to her and the possible threat of her presence since the incident in the clearing. She had been grateful to be delivered from the hands of Curly Hyde and Walt Crow, but that was over and done with, and the situation between her and Luke had doubtless changed—but to what extent he could only hazard a guess.

"Two, maybe three days—by horseback."

Braden glanced irritably at the marshal. "How the hell else can we go?"

Rye was bearing in mind the existence of Pete Stanley and his friends. They had made no effort to get at Braden since the cabin near Galena Crossing, but his vigilance where the outlaws were concerned was sharpening as the distance to Yuma Prison decreased. They would be waiting somewhere ahead in that final stretch of empty, savage land, he was certain.

He was casting about for some means of crossing the desert without drawing their notice. The idea of going straight on, chancing a showdown, was finding no favor with him. Not that he harbored any personal fear of a confrontation, but Pete Stanley was no fool; he likely had already sought out a vantage point where he and the others could cover the road, and in such wide open country there was little a man could do to protect himself from long-range rifles.

Whatever, the first step must be to eliminate any possible danger Zoe Braden might pose. Continuing to ignore the outlaw's peevish question, he turned to her.

"Be coming to a town about noon tomorrow. Place called Arroyo Largo. I'll leave you there."

She was silent for a few moments. Then, "You may need help—later. If I could have my gun—"

Rye considered her words. The break between Zoe and Luke appeared definite, irrevocable, but he couldn't be sure of it. They were husband and wife, and despite the bitterness that had passed between them the girl could still feel a sense of obligation. Too, it could all have been staged for his benefit.

"It Pete and them others you're worrying about?" Braden asked.

Rye nodded. "They won't give it up until you're inside the walls of Yuma."

Luke swore raggedly. "Reckon I'm a goner any way you look at it. Everybody's against me. . . . Just don't have a chance."

The lawman slid a covert glance at the woman, saw a fleeting look of sympathy cross her face, vanish as quickly. His thoughts on the matter crystallized; he wouldn't trust her—dared not. At some critical, opportune moment she might turn against him.

"This here town, maybe you can get some help there," Luke said, hopefully.

"Only a way station. Couple or three houses, a dozen people at the most. Water stop's about all it is."

"Then you sure better listen to Zoe—"

Rye shook his head. "No, I'm leaving her there."

23

Arroyo Largo was all but deserted when they rode in next day around midmorning. An old prospector camped beside the spring told Rye that the few others who had lived there when the place was a regular stop for the stagecoach had moved on when the line changed to a different route.

The abandoning of the stage stop came as a surprise to the lawman. Disappointed, he stood motionless, staring out across the desert shimmering in the heat. His plan for the remainder of the journey, devised during the night, entailed borrowing or renting a buckboard or wagon for the use of Braden and himself and passing themselves off to the outlaws as pilgrims heading west. Very possibly it would have worked, but it was obviously out of the question now and he had no choice but to continue on as before—and with Zoe Braden still on his hands.

"You see four riders pass through here in the last couple of days?" he asked, turning to the prospector.

Nearby the girl was refilling their canteens while the horses slaked their thirsts.

"Maybe," the old man replied, not taking his eyes off her.

Rye impatiently lifted the flap of his shirt pocket, displayed the gold-finished marshal's badge he wore.

"Not the kind of an answer I want!" he snapped. "Four men. One's a redhead. All hard-lookers."

The prospector's stooped shoulders stirred. "Yeh, reckon I did. Was yesterday morning—early. They laid around here for a couple of hours, then rode off."

"Going on towards Yuma?"

"What they done. . . . You chasing them, Marshal?"

"Dodging them," the lawman said in a show of wry humor.

A puzzled look crossed the old man's bearded face, but Rye, making no further explanation, swung back onto the chestnut, and, bucking his head at Zoe and Luke, cut through the thin stand of trees and rejoined the road.

"What're you aiming to do?" Braden demanded as they lined up abreast on the dusty course. "You just going to ride right into them, let them—?"

"My problem. I'll handle it," the lawman said. "You do what I tell you. That's all you need to think about."

"Where do I stand?" Zoe asked, leaning forward on her saddle to see past Luke.

"Nothing's changed," Rye said gruffly. "You're here because I had no place to leave you."

They continued on for the better part of an hour and then the lawman began to swing away from the deeply cut ruts of the once well-traveled route and angle for a fairly wide arroyo paralleling it. As they rode down into the loose sand, Luke Braden at once voiced his objections.

"You best think of something better'n this! A man can

see for forty mile in this damned country, so we ain't going to be able to do no hiding."

Rye could not deny the statement but there was nothing else to be done other than take advantage of whatever bit of cover was offered them. Scattered here and there in the miles ahead were small clusters of hills, all well separated and offering protection from view only to anyone already in them. Pete and his men could be hiding in one such group, he knew, waiting patiently for them to appear.

Which range of hills would the outlaws be most likely to choose? Being almost two days in front of them, Stanley would have ample time in which to make the right selection. Rye raked his memory, tried to recall the road, the country bordering it. Where would a man find the best spot to lay an ambush and still be far enough from Yuma Prison and the town not to attract lawmen or any of the soldiers in the small garrison stationed along the river?

The Pass—this side of it. It came to the marshal in a sudden recollection. To reach the settlement with its nearby prison, travelers must cross a low range of hills called the Gila Mountains. A cut through the sun-seared, blackened formations had been established for the convenience of the stage lines as well as pilgrims, enabling them more easily to attain their destination, some twenty miles farther on.

Rye gave it deep thought. The Pass was where the outlaws would be waiting; it was the logical point, and, with that conviction in his mind, he began to plan ahead with countering measures. He'd keep well south of the usual route, approach the Gilas a considerable distance below the cut. He was unable to recall if it was possible to cross the rugged formation at any alternate point or not, having used only the established course in the three or four times when he had traveled through that part of the country; but it would pay to search for one.

Also, they'd make that last leg of the trip at night. Not only would it be safer but it would be easier on the horses, which, by the time they had crossed that lengthy stretch of desert, would be in far from good condition and unable to withstand a hard, fast run should it become necessary.

They camped that night in a narrow canyon on the slope of a solitary hill, using their water sparingly since there would be no possibility of replenishing their supply until they reached Yuma. Rye made no mention of his plans, as was his custom, but Zoe, staring out over the hushed, deceptively beautiful land, put the matter squarely to him.

"Our chances of reaching Yuma aren't good, are they—?"

The lawman, engaged in filling the empty loops of his gun belt with cartridges, did not look up. "Could be better."

"Do you have to take Luke there? Isn't there some other town you could go to first and get help? We know those outlaws are out there—just sitting and waiting to kill us all."

"No other towns around. It has to be Yuma. . . . We'll make it through. I'm not about to ride straight into them."

"But how—if it's the only road—?"

"Aim to come in from the lower end of the Gilas. They won't be expecting us to show up there. It'll let me spot them before they do us."

"But if you don't?"

Finished with the belt, Rye got to his feet, crossed to where he had laid out his saddle. "I'll know in time," he said, digging about in one of the leather pouches for shotgun shells. Producing a handful, he distributed them among his pockets.

The girl sighed heavily, moved slowly off into the cooling rocks. Abruptly her voice came back to him.

"Marshal—there's a campfire—"

Rye pivoted, hurried to where she stood.

"There—near those little hills," Zoe said, pointing into the distance. "Could that be them?"

The lawman studied the small, red eye winking faintly in the darkness. It was a campfire, there was no doubt of that—and it could be Pete Stanley. Just as possibly it could be Indians, a prospector or party of pilgrims. The glow was not far off the main road and near to a line of fair-sized hills called the Mohawks by most. Anyone following the established route to Yuma would pass along the extreme north end of the formations.

Stanley could have set his ambush there; unaware of the Pass in the Gilas, he could have chosen the first opportune location encountered along the trail. At once Rye dropped back to the camp. Braden, chained to a thick clump of greasewood, was snoring noisily on his blanket. The lawman shook him awake.

"You know if Pete or any of that bunch with him knows this part of the country?"

Luke stared at Rye dumbly, not understanding. The marshal repeated the question, finally got through.

"How the hell would I know? Don't think so. They done their riding up Kansas way—and Colorado and New Mexico, seems. Why?"

The lawman turned away, walked slowly to where the horses were picketed. The day had been long and hot and all three were showing its effects. He felt Zoe at his elbow.

"What is it, John? What does it mean?"

It was the first time she had called him by his first name and it brought a faint smile to his lips. Few persons ever took the liberty.

"Good chance that's Stanley out there."

She looked off toward the distant spot of light. "How far away is it?"

"Twenty miles, maybe more. Fire shows up a long ways on a clear night like this one."

Zoe was quiet, listening to the squeaking of a pack rat or some other small animal back in the rocks while she waited for him to continue.

"We'll gamble on it being Pete," he said finally. "Horses are tired now but if we hold off for a few hours, let them rest, they'll be in shape to pull out, get us past the camp before first light."

"What if it's not Stanley?"

"Be no worse off than we are now. . . . Get some sleep. We'll move on around midnight."

24

Under other circumstances it would have been a pleasant ride across the desert in the cool, pale moonlight. Large white flowers that hid themselves in the day from the sun's scorching rays were now fully spread, their sweetness perfuming the air and attracting myriads of large moths and other insects.

Clumps of snakeweed, desert broom and other shrubs took on a silver sheen and even the gaunt chollas and occasional joshua yuccas appeared less bleak and formidable. At times birds hurtled out from beneath the horses' hooves, startled by their passage, drawing the attention of a thick-bodied owl on one such occasion that launched itself into immediate pursuit with a soft swishing of broad wings from a mesquite.

All was lost on a dozing Luke, but Zoe, riding at John Rye's left, missed none of it.

"Everything's so different at night," she murmured. "It's like another world, so quiet and calm—even beautiful."

The lawman nodded. "All of that, for sure—but the desert can kill you if you let down your guard."

She turned to him, an odd expression on her face. In the muted light her skin had a creamy look, and her eyes appeared larger, darker.

"Is death always on your mind? It seems to be the first thing in your thoughts."

Gaze locked to the distant campfire, Rye gave the question deliberate consideration. "Could be," he said after a while. "Kind of work I'm in puts it always at my shoulder. If I ever forgot it—how quick and easy it can come—I'd likely end up dead."

Zoe shivered. "It's as if you dealt in death—"

"Guess maybe I do. Men I'm sent to bring in are marked for it."

"And sometimes you have to kill them before you're through—before the law gets to have its way."

"Sometimes." His voice had grown cool. "I have the right to protect myself against them if it becomes necessary. Same goes for their friends."

She was quiet for a long minute. Then, "It's a terrible way to live. . . . I guess I understand better now why people call you what they do—the Doomsday Marshal. I feel sorry for you."

"Don't. Save it for somebody who needs it," Rye said stiffly, "like your husband there when he's swinging from the gallows."

They rode on in silence after that, following out the shallow arroyos, avoiding the occasional rises that lifted, like small domes, from the flat desert land. The lawman doubted they could be seen by Pete Stanley and his men, if they were the ones at the campfire, but as always he took nothing for granted.

The small, red eye died out, became as the rest of the night, but its location had become fixed in the marshal's mind and with that specific point at the upper, rocky end of the Mohawks established, he bore steadily toward it. He had no plan other than to get past the outlaws without drawing their attention. His general knowledge of the country, however, was not sufficient for him to know if he could lead his prisoner and the girl through the ragged hills below the campsite undetected or not. Such was what he hoped to do, and if successful a showdown with Pete Stanley and the men who sided him would be averted.

Shortly before first light they reached the Mohawks and were moving slowly along the foot of the rough, irregular range. Rye, searching the formation for some indication of a trail that would permit them to pass through without endangering the horses, felt his hopes sag as they drew near the upper end. Finally he lifted a hand, signaled for a halt. At once Zoe, who had dropped back to ride alongside Luke, spurred up to him.

"What is it?"

"The camp'll be on the other side of that shoulder," he said, pointing to a bulge of rock a hundred yards or so on ahead. "Have to take our chances from here on."

The girl frowned. "But won't they see us?"

"Aim to circle wide. . . . There was no place we could've cut through. Too risky for the horses."

Zoe was studying him thoughtfully in the cool grayness. "I think you knew it would be this way all along."

"Meaning?"

"You want to face those outlaws—shoot it out with them."

The line of John Rye's jaw hardened. Reaching down

he drew the shotgun from its oiled boot, laid it across his legs. She was overlooking the fact that he wasn't even certain it was Stanley's camp—besides ignoring the obvious odds he would be up against if it were. But he let it drop.

"Sure, if you say so," he murmured.

Twisting half about, he stared off to their right. "I can see an arroyo cutting in toward the hills over there. We'll double back, drop into it. If it's deep enough, we'll be able to skirt the camp without being seen."

"What if it's not?"

A hard smile pulled at his lips. "Seems you've already got it figured," he said, shrugging, and, looping Braden's lead rope about his saddle horn, headed for the wash.

It was not deep, Rye saw that when they drew close and began to move down into it, but there was no alternative. Looking back over his shoulder, he beckoned to the girl.

"Stay up close," he said when she was beside him. "If anything starts, ride straight on 'til you come to the road —then keep going. It'll take you to Yuma."

His tone made it clear it was not an indication of interest in her welfare on his part but a simple outlining of the direction she should follow to reach civilization, should it become necessary. Zoe nodded.

He held the chestnut to a slow walk, almost soundless as the loose sand muffled the thud of hooves. Shotgun resting on his lap, he kept his eyes fixed on the jutting point of the hills, awaiting the moment when he would have his first glimpse of the camp—and the horses.

If there were four mounts he would assume it was the

outlaws. There could be a party of pilgrims, or Indians, in that like number of course, but the chances were all against it. There were many better places along the road where a traveler could pull up for the night; only someone with a definite purpose in mind would be likely to choose the tip of the unfriendly-looking Mohawks.

Four horses . . . Rye saw them, picketed well back in a narrow side canyon just below the point. From the road they could not be seen, nor could the camp itself, which was placed behind a large spill of boulders.

"It's them," he said in a low voice. "Still asleep. We go easy."

There was no response from the girl or from Luke Braden. They continued on, the horses plodding at a slow gait while behind them, far beyond the ragged horizon in the east, dawn was throwing an aurora of color into the sky.

They drew abreast of the camp, moved past the hillock of rocks that at some time in the past had come plunging down from higher levels to form a sort of ring at the base of the mountain. The arroyo began to flatten out, merge with ground level. The lawman, cool, the planes of his face tightly drawn, neither slowed nor quickened the pace of the horses but held to the same methodic gait.

It seemed strange to him that Stanley had not put a man on watch, one stationed at some high point where he could observe the road and be aware of anyone approaching from the east, but he could find no sign of a sentry. It could be the outlaw was not expecting them until later in the day and deemed such precaution at that early hour unnecessary.

A rifle shot suddenly blasted the hush. Dust spurted up a few strides to John Rye's left as a yell sounded in the camp. He'd been wrong; there was a sentry.

"Get out of here!" he shouted as Zoe spurred up to him.

Giving her no further thought, he jerked hard on the black's lead rope, bringing Braden to his side. "Keep down and in close—if you don't want to stop a bullet!" he warned the outlaw, and roweled the chestnut.

The big horse leaped ahead. Braden's black lagged briefly and then broke into a matching gallop. More shots were coming from the rocks and the sound of bullets thunking into the sand and clipping through the brush clumps was all around them.

"We ain't got a chance!" Luke yelled in a frantic voice.

Grim, the marshal leaned forward and slid the shotgun back into its scabbard. The moments when it would have been effective were past, gone when they moved beyond the camp and out of the weapon's range. Drawing his pistol, Rye crouched low and glanced over his shoulder.

The outlaws, aroused and now mounted, were streaming down from the rocks. On higher, sloping ground they were closing fast, withholding their fire, apparently intent only on interception. Rye came back around. They had broken out of the arroyo, leaving behind its unstable footing, were turning onto the solid surface of the road. Some distance on ahead he could see Zoe.

Stanley and the other outlaws were now at a direct right angle to him, and as the chestnut began to lengthen his stride, the lawman squared himself on the saddle. Allowing the leathers to hang from the horn, he crooked his left elbow, steadied his pistol on his forearm and leveled it at the nearest of the riders racing toward him in a tight group. He pressed off the shot. The outlaw threw up his arms, and went off his horse backwards.

"You got him!" Braden yelled gleefully. "By God, give me that there gun of Zoe's and I'll—"

The outlaws resumed their firing. Rye glanced at Luke. "Keep down!" he shouted, and again triggered his weapon.

A second rider slowed, hand going to his shoulder as he began to swing away from the others.

"That was Amos—Amos Cook!" Braden yelled. "You winged him!"

A bullet ripped into the blanket roll behind the cantle of Rye's saddle. Another clipped the brim of his flat-crowned hat. Seemingly oblivious, he again braced the pistol on his forearm as the chestnut pounded along the road.

A third bullet plucked at the lawman's sleeve, left a trace of blood on his wrist. He flinched slightly, triggered his weapon once more. The outlaw in line with its sights jolted, rocked to one side and then began to fall from his horse.

"That was Pete!" Braden shouted. "You got Pete Stanley!"

Rye scarcely heard as he trained his weapon on the fourth man—but there was no target. The outlaw had wheeled off sharply as Stanley tumbled from his saddle and was spurring toward the hills and his wounded partner.

"Which one was that?" Rye asked tautly, reloading as the chestnut began to slacken his headlong flight.

"Ollie King—"

"The other?"

"The one you winged? Was Ben Polk."

Ben Polk . . . Ollie King . . . He'd remember their names. They were the last of the gang that had been with Braden in the bank holdup and the killings. The law would now know their identities and take steps to bring them in. Holstering his weapon, he looked on down the road. Zoe had halted, dismounted and was waiting for them at the edge of a brushy wash that cut across the twin ruts. Not too far beyond her lay the Gilas and then would come Yuma and the prison—and the end of the job.

They reached the girl, and, nodding coolly to her, Rye pulled to a stop. The horses were trembling from the hard, fast run and glistening with sweat. They would need to rest before undertaking the final miles. Swinging down, the lawman ground-reined the chestnut, walked toward Braden. Keyed wire taut from the preceding minutes of surging violence, tension had not yet completely drained from him and he still moved in a deliberate, coiled sort of way.

"Marshal—I'm sorry to do—"

At the sound of Zoe Braden's portentous words John Rye reacted instinctively and without conscious thought. His hand swept down, came up as he pivoted. The blast of his gun drowned the girl's scream as she threw herself to one side, dropping the twin-barreled derringer she had hoarded so carefully inside her boot for all those many days.

He stood for a long breath, a crouched, threatening shape staring at her, and then as she drew herself erect, untouched by his bullet, his hunched shoulders relented. Holstering his weapon, he picked up the derringer, hurled it off into the brush and faced her.

"You'll never come any closer to dying," he said in a low, furious voice.

Zoe shook her head. "I—I had to try."

The lawman continued to study her, his deep-set eyes hard, bitter.

"You got any more tricks up your sleeve?"

"No—that ends it. I—"

"Damn you!" Luke shouted, recovering from his surprise. "Might've knowed you'd mess up the only chance you'll be getting! Now how d'you expect to—?"

The outlaw, his eyes lifting, reaching out beyond the girl and the marshal, allowed his words to trail off. A slow smile spread across his face.

"Howdy, Linus," he said.

25

Rye stiffened. Linus . . . Linus Kirby . . . The deputy.

"Don't be trying to draw, Rye," Boston City's one-time lawman warned in a high, nervous voice. "You ain't dealing with no woman this time, and I ain't going to get caught flat-footed like she was."

"Pull that trigger, Deputy! Pull that trigger!" Luke Braden shouted wildly. "Get it done like you claimed you was going to do!"

"Put your hands up. Turn around—slow," Kirby said, seeming not to hear the outlaw.

Rye lifted his arms, wheeled gently. Pistol cocked and leveled, Kirby was standing at the edge of the arroyo where he'd apparently been waiting in the brush. The skin of his face was stretched tight and his mouth twitched from the strain that gripped him.

"Go ahead—get it done!" Braden urged.

A dry smile pulled at the marshal's lips. "You aiming to just shoot me down?"

Patches of sweat on Kirby's cheekbones shone dully. "Nope, not exactly. Going to let you go for your gun."

"While you're standing there with your piece already cocked?"

"Sure. If you're such a ring-tailed wonder like everybody says, I figure it'll be about even steven—you drawing faster'n I can pull the trigger."

"You're a fool, Linus!" Zoe said. "You don't know what you're trying to do."

"I sure do—I'm settling a little score. Rode all the way down here from Boston City for just that."

"He'll kill you. He'll manage it, somehow."

"Got my doubts about that."

"Zoe's right!" Luke shouted desperately. "Best you cut out the fancy stuff and start shooting!"

"Listen to her," Rye said in his low, quiet way. "That pride of yours will make a dead man out of you."

"You ain't bluffing me—"

"Not trying to. Just don't want to kill you."

"Ain't likely you will—not with me holding a gun on you. All I got to do is pull the trigger."

The lawman smiled bleakly. "You won't have that much time."

"Stop it!" Zoe cried suddenly, and stepped in between the two men. "There's been too much killing already on account of Luke—and I won't have any more of it! You hear—both of you? Linus, put that gun away or I'll make you use it on me!"

The younger man frowned uncertainly. "By God, if you—"

Zoe abruptly crossed to him, stood with her body against the muzzle of his pistol. "I mean it! I'm sick of killing—I won't stand for any more."

Rye had lowered his arms, was watching, faint amusement in his eyes. Braden was sitting slackly in his saddle cursing the girl and Kirby in a steady, monotonous voice.

Linus shifted nervously, allowed his weapon to sag.
After a time he slid it back into its holster, obvious relief filling his eyes as he looked past the girl to Rye.

"There'll be another day," he said, mustering a hard
tone.

The lawman shook his head. "Doubt that—you're not
the kind," he said. "Now, how about giving me a hand
taking my prisoner on to Yuma? . . . Just might find yourself a good job there."

It was late in the afternoon when John Rye rode
through the prison gate and halted on the barren, rocky
surface outside the wall. Luke Braden was safely locked
in a cell, and Linus Kirby had found work as a guard.

Brushing away the sweat on his face, the marshal
reached into a pocket and drew out a letter the warden
had delivered to him on his arrival. From headquarters, it
directed him to report to the governor of Texas at Austin,
where another job awaited. He considered the creased
sheet of paper for several moments, put it back in its place
as his thoughts shifted to Zoe.

What was it she had said when he'd asked her where
she would go? *To the nearest town and the biggest saloon*
—that had been her answer. Roweling the chestnut, Rye
started down the slope for Yuma. That's where he'd be
for the next few days, too. . . . The governor of Texas
would have to be patient. He needed a few days off.